INHERIT THE TIDE

A NOVEL BY
KEN BOIRE

Outskirts Press, Inc.
Denver, Colorado

This is a work of fiction. The events and characters described here are imaginary and are not intended to refer to specific places or living persons. The opinions expressed in this manuscript are solely the opinions of the author and do not represent the opinions or thoughts of the publisher. The author represents and warrants that s/he either owns or has the legal right to publish all material in this book. If you believe this to be incorrect, contact the publisher through its website at www.outskirtspress.com.

Inherit the Tide

Outskirts Press
http://www.outskirtspress.com

ISBN-10: 1-59800-152-3
ISBN-13: 978-1-59800-152-5

Library of Congress Control Number 2005935079

Printed in the United States of America

Published for
The American Arts and Literature Project
Printed and Distributed by
Outskirts Press Inc, Denver Colorado.

Cover Photography by Bushnell Digital Imaging
PO Box 355, Bremerton WA 98337

Foreword

During preparation of the manuscript, early drafts were looked at by experienced editors, authors, and agents. Hopefully their early comments will mirror the reader's reaction to this finished version of the novel.

"A captivating story set in the Pacific Northwest...attention-grabbing...involved."

"Realistic characters that come alive on the page…"

"Strong story, interesting characters…"

"Obviously well researched…"

"A well developed, carefully woven story linking the characters from front to back..."

"Excellent work and interesting to read…good story."

"An interesting and pretty story."

"Possible future Book Award candidate"

"Powerful without gutter talk, violence, or gratuitous sex... a good book out of a 21st century writer."

A growing friendship between Grandma and her ten-year-old, half Indian grandson set the stage. This story takes the reader from an Arctic expedition in the 1860s to present day Seattle. Two stories unfold nearly a century apart, one centering on Grandma and the other on the boy. Grandma's story leads the reader through pioneer Seattle as a rough edged timber town, then to 1950 and beyond. The boy understands Grandma's story from the point of view of a ten-year-old growing up in Seattle.

Events seen from two different perspectives link Grandma's story to the real life, present day adventures of the boy. He experiences a growing awareness of the power of the tide in his Indian heritage. The story explores awareness of the cultural gap between Indians and others from the view of two different generations. Entwined in the story are prostitutes, city founders, Indian tribes, Chief Seattle, and Arctic adventurers. This is a story of adventure, conflict, failure, and triumph built on the Indian legend that we are what we believe and understand.

CHAPTER 1

Seeding the Tide

Regal, and time worn, her downcast eyes seemed to be unaware of my presence. She arose, walked to the cook stove, and bent over to rattle the grate then threw three small shovels of coal into the fire. She gripped the steel handle of the shovel tightly in her bare hand, even though it was hot from being stuffed in the coal bucket between the wall and the stove. She straightened her back and brought her head and chin high in the soft morning light streaming through the small window over the kitchen door. The beam of light was dulled by the aged glass and the shadow of a porch roof which ringed the faded white house all the way around.

Looking at her I wondered for a moment what was going on in her head. Was she thinking about the Arctic coast of Alaska and the legends about ships that have come to grief in the crush of ice and fierce storms? She had promised me a story about how over the last two hundred years there have been so many losses of great ships and capable crews, a small city could be populated by these talented men and women. I was chilled by how she said the graveyard of steel, wood, and flesh reaches well over a thousand miles, across the Bering Sea to north of the Arctic Circle. What stories there must be I thought.

Firelight from inside the stove glowed against her high cheekbones and flashed off her hair – once black, still wavy – which was for all occasions pulled back into a single long braid that fell nearly to her waist. The fire burned brighter and higher. The light reflected off her wet shoes, which looked like a man's and seemed too big for the tiny wiry body above them.

She stirred, then smiled at me and I knew she had been aware of my presence probably since I had approached the kitchen. I felt she was thanking me for letting her have time with her thoughts. She retied her apron and moved her brown hands as if to smooth her hair, then reached out and closed the iron door. Turning toward me, barely inches taller, she ran her fingers through my hair. “Probably the only part of you that doesn’t hurt. With hair and eyes like this, you should have been a girl. Would be a lot less worry for me I’m thinking.” She kissed me on the forehead, to which I said, “Ouch,” but didn’t wipe it off.

She guided me backwards to a kitchen chair where she had already placed two pillows in preparation for my aching body. We sat together and watched white and yellow flames lick at the hinges and cracks around the edges of the door where years of use had eaten away the floral relief pattern cast into the iron. This had been long before I was born. Warmth began to drive away the dampness. She rose again and filled a pan with water then put it on the stove. As water droplets sizzled the pan began to dance and rock by itself and she sat down again.

I waited for hot cocoa and fresh, toasted, homemade bread. I rested my plaster cast on the table and tried to make myself comfortable, but I was sore and aching from head to toe and inside the cast my newly broken arm hurt a lot.

Grandma was quiet for a long time and then gave me that look, and I knew something good was about to come out of her mouth. She was a great storyteller. I never knew if the next sentence was going to be her talking like a sailor, preacher, or college professor. Normally, I would not have the patience to listen for as long as she could talk, being a fidgety kid with the world to conquer. But my broken arm put me in an entirely different frame of mind and I wanted to take my mind off of myself. God, I felt so stupid now. My choices were pretty limited and a story might help since I couldn’t ride a bike, hit or throw a baseball, swim, or even play tag. Right now, I hurt all over but what bothered me most was the feeling stupid part. Yup, I did this to myself. I had that lump in the throat feeling, sort of an ache inside that was all over me, and I wanted it to go away. I just felt like crying but not because of the hurt, but because I did it to myself and now everybody knew. I couldn't shake that feeling about wishing I could just crawl down an ant hole for a while.

She said, "Remember when we went to the rodeo in Yakima and all those cowboys got bucked into the dust and horse poop? Try to remember if you saw any of them pick up his hat and go home. Every one of them got back on another horse and did their best to stick it out, one hand in the air, yelling and all, like having the funnest time of his life. Getting bucked off in front of four thousand people has to hurt a cowboy even if nothing gets broken. They don't show up to land in the dust you know. Every one of those cowpokes got back on and there was some pretty damn big horses there. You haven't seen any big horses bucking under you in your life yet, so just start thinking about getting back on instead of thinking about how much it hurts to get bucked off. You just had an adventure with old Broken Top you're going to remember the rest of your life, and that fits in this family just about perfect.

"Hecky, I know what your thinking and I know what you're feeling and neither on of 'em is right. Part of being a kid is doing stuff you've never done before. That is where the fun of life comes from, so long as nobody gets hurt of course. Well your hurtin', but so what, everybody else is okay and you will be too – life goes on. Nothing wrong with being a kid, nothing wrong with doing new things, nothing wrong with adventure, there is only something wrong if it changes you into Wimpyboy." I sort of snorted, almost laughed at that because she knew my hero was Superboy in the comics I collected. Jeez, my ribs hurt. I had this vision of a chubby kid with glasses and a cape that chased little loose horses but never caught any.

She went on, "Actually, it might have been a good thing in some ways. There won't be any lasting damage, and who knows, you might even become wiser and stronger." The first part caused the low feeling inside of me to start going away. Nothing wrong, with me? I really needed to hear that, I guess. Cowboys? Jeez they were my real life heroes. The last part, about becoming wiser and stronger had me confused, but I was thinking she said that not wanting an answer, so I ignored it. Still wondering how stuff that doesn't kill you makes you wiser and stronger, I asked, "I'm not goofy, stupid or crazy then?"

"No Hecky, you're ten. You're a boy. You're strong and smart. You're part of our family and heaven knows we have done our share of adventurous things, so I guess that item with Broken Top was in your blood. You probably couldn't have done anything else."

"How can being ten be in your blood."

"No, I mean being the adventurous kid that you are, is in your blood like, being smart, liking to be with others, looking for challenges, and so on. I know your spirit was delivered to us on the wind and tide. I have felt that for a long time you are a connection for me." She looked me straight in the eye, and in the sparkle I knew there was going to be a story starting right there at the kitchen table.

She ruffled the pillow behind me and placed a cup of hot cocoa in front of me and combed her fingers through my hair again. I didn't hurt inside anymore. "Grandson, I will tell you how you have the spirit of the wind and tide, and why you are strong like the sea. Your history is rich with adventure and triumph but also has brushes with ne'er-do-wells, criminals, and outright failures. This story starts about one hundred years ago, far away, to the north of here in the high Arctic near the top of the world. It has adventure, love, and hate. Listen carefully, for this is your story and someday you must tell it to another generation, too." She leaned back in her chair, close to my side now, with shoes off and stocking feet extended past mine toward the cook stove, and began her story in her warm, low voice, a cello.

That rainy morning was fifty-five years ago and the story you are about to hear was told to me by Grandma when I was a boy living on Denny Hill above Elliot Bay. It is the first time the story has been committed to the printed word.

CHAPTER 2

Before the Story

In those days of my childhood, automobiles were huge with fat white tires, our city had a baseball team with the same name as the town's best beer, cigars were sold and smoked wherever there were barbershops, and street corners had sailors who whistled at girls who liked the attention, suddenly standing tall in their tight skirts and heels. Comics were a dime, and in those days the life of most kids in the city was good, and for me, very good.

It was not yet 1950 and I was seeing the world through the eyes of a ten-year-old and I loved it all. To me, even then it was like living inside of a movie. There were all sorts of characters, and now that I look back there were stories within stories. The lessons they could have taught are not necessarily the kinds of things a ten-year-old figures out. I never stopped trying to unravel things at the time, and often the riddle of how experiences were all supposed to fit together was the last thing I would think of at night as I drifted off to sleep. Some parts I just sort of gave up on, like why I used to be uncomfortable around old people. I'm not really sure why I felt that way but it sort of went away as I got to know Grandma better. For some reason, I never thought of her as old.

Funny what you remember about being ten. Some things never leave your brain. Of course I still have some kid memories I do not fully understand but they don't really bother me. Like back then, a lot of nights I was uneasy around bedtime, in my attic bedroom. Maybe I was scared by a dream I kept having about being surrounded by old people. I never figured out for sure where this baseball field was in the dream. But the dream always started by me looking from the outfield at the bleachers full of unfamiliar faces. They grew older and older by the second. Then they reached out for me, closing in, stumbling and falling. Like a chorus of violins, I heard them singing my name. Everybody was in military regalia, some with bandages and missing limbs.

In the dream, my kid's baseball uniform grew old and tattered while I was wearing it. Then I saw myself screaming for help to a brightly lit man in a crinkly new baseball uniform hitting fly balls to an empty outfield. The batter turned to face me and it was Dad. In a flash of spreading light I was back in a brand new baseball uniform as the rest of the dream changed to a flow of dancing rainbow colors and piano waltzes.

I never told anyone about the dream. I really didn't like the first part because it scared me so much I didn't like sleeping upstairs alone, especially if I had a bad day. But I was afraid if I told anyone I wouldn't have it anymore and that would mean I wouldn't see Dad again.

The world felt normal when Grandma was around. The day Grandma came to town to live with us, I was excited, sort of like how I got waiting for presents on Christmas morning, anxious and giddy. You know, sort of the way when you just can't sit or stand in one place for more than a few seconds. The day was warm for early spring. I was at the corner on my bike waiting for her taxi, and raced the cab to the house. The cab rattled past me and skidded to a stop on the gravel. As the driver was fumbling with change, I dropped the bike, opened the car door and reached in for her bag. The leather suitcase was heavier than I thought one ought to be and I staggered, forcing a smile, up toward the front porch. I thought she was right behind me so I struggled up the stairs tight lipped, then at the top looked over my shoulder to see the taxi drive off, then I saw Grandma's blue flowered dress and open coat flapping, peddling the bike up the driveway. One foot down, she spun around in the loose gravel and yelled, "Hecky, watch this." She took her hands off the handlebars and coasted to the street.

As she swooped back to the curb I ran out to meet her, glad for a reason to leave the suitcase on the porch. She stood straight as a rail and had a laugh that could blanket the hillside. Sometimes in the summer from my tree house behind the carriage barn it would ring throughout the old house. I was the only kid in the neighborhood who had a grandma who could throw a football and ride a bike with no hands.

Mom said Grandma needed us to be near her after Grandpa died. She said the house was really Grandma's, anyway, because her dad was the one who had built it eighty years before. The house was the place Grandma lived when she was growing up, so she was really coming back home.

So, Grandma sort of came full circle. Fifteen years earlier when Grandpa was alive they moved out of the house in the city to a beach cabin on an island in the sound. Their beach place was just a few miles across the water from Seattle but there was no bridge so seemed a lot farther. The cabin really looked like it belonged at the beach with rough shake siding and a huge stone fireplace. On the side that faced the beach there were a bunch of small windows from floor to ceiling. Some of them worked like doors but even with everything closed up the place was drafty. I guess that's why there always seemed to be a fire going.

The cabin was tucked away in the firs about two miles north of the weather worn ferry dock. You had to go down a dirt road, past hills dotted with a checkerboard of strawberry farms and houses. The farms looked like the cardboard cutouts in the farm set I got for Christmas when I was seven. Along the road, some of the farm gates had names I couldn't read. Grandma said they were written in Japanese. Japanese families had owned them before the war, she said, and before the internment, whatever that was. Everybody said that when the war was all over few of them had anything left worth coming back to.

You could see they were nice farms laid out tight and neat, just like the ones you could see on Christmas cards and magazine covers. What you couldn't see was how sad things were for almost everybody. During the war, Grandpa and Grandma tried real hard to take care of the farms the Japanese people left behind. She said, "It's what you do for friends and what they would do for us." I knew they harvested what they could and used the crop money for payments and taxes. But if you can't do everything needed to care for a farm or anything else, you can't really expect a farm to take care of you. It must have been pretty clear two old people couldn't make a dent in all of the things that needed to be done. The details were beyond me but I knew they couldn't pay all of the bills.

Grandma was a tough old bird and I was surprised when she said she begged the bankers, but before the war was over most of the farms got taken away. Other people on the island were waiting to buy up the farms from the bankers. Somehow though, a few of the Japanese without large payments were able to keep ahead of the taxes and keep their farms. So after the war Grandma and Grandpa still had some Japanese neighbors.

The few families who still owned property gave shelter to the ones who were not so fortunate. Crowded together, each house seemed like one huge family, happy, bonded, full of life at the end of the work day. Grandma said, "Hard work has value to them. Since they value work, work gives them dignity and respect. They get up at dawn and welcome the rising sun, then they raise the American flag. Even the ones that had lost sons and husbands serving in the U.S. military during the war join the flag ceremony. I think we could all learn something from them. We could learn a lot."

When Dad's plane was shot down in the Pacific three days before the end of the war, Grandma and Grandpa told me later that they wrote letters to their Japanese friends in the camps in Idaho. I wasn't even in first grade yet and I didn't remember much about the day we found out he was dead. I think people tried to protect me from what had happened. I just remember how sad everybody was and all the visitors we had at the house. Grandma and Grandpa wanted their Japanese friends to know too.

After the war, not much time went by before they started showing up at the island ferry dock. In my kid memory I remember them bent against the early fall wind and rain, struggling with tattered bundles. They were a rag-tag bunch in clothing so badly worn that you could not say what colors some of them were wearing. I was six years old when Grandma and Grandpa took me down there to meet them.

After the ferry landed Grandma bowed to each one of the arriving Japanese as they stepped onto the dock. She said something to them in the few words of Japanese she had learned before the war. Then she grabbed them and hugged them only the way Grandma could do. The other islanders on the ferry dock stepped back in silent knots as the Japanese closed in around her like a fortress wall.

I remember feeling the dock move gently under us in the cold early time before dawn. We looked toward the East, hoping the sun would show itself, but the clouds extended to the horizon. Gusts from across the bay drove rain in our faces, throwing hard waves against the dock. The planks shuddered, sending salt water into the air. As they gathered Grandma, Grandpa and I into their tight huddle, I could see men and women with tears on their faces, or maybe just the rain. Nobody spoke for a long time. There were Japanese kids my age there too. They seemed afraid of something. I couldn't get them to talk. They didn't answer even when I asked them their favorite baseball team, just smiled. And when I asked if they had a million dollars what they would do with it, they just sort of looked at their feet. I asked one of the boys if he wanted to go fishing with us and that was the key. From that time on I had a genuine fishing partner even though all we caught off the old ferry dock that summer were bullheads. Some of the littlest kids were born in Idaho and were just now coming home.

Penned up in the middle of Idaho, they had never seen much water before and I thought it was more than they could take in at one time.

The island cabin sat in the shade of evergreens on a cliff edge, high above the gray beach. The dirt road beyond the first berry farms became narrower in the woods. If two cars met, one had to back up until they found a place wide enough to squeeze past. Neighbors rarely saw each other because they enjoyed the privacy of the thick forest and remote beach. Houses along the beach were scattered widely apart, so people knew names but saw each other mostly at the meetings on the road. Most meetings were just a short howdy between car windows. With two wheels crushing through the tangle of roadside ferns, vines scratching at the fenders and doors, the drivers waved, smiled, said, "How ya doin?" then they were past and it was over. Only my Grandma's meetings on the road were long. Stuck there, I couldn't help but think of grazing cattle for some reason. People wanted to talk to her, and every time I knew we would be stopped there in the road, until somebody else needed to get by.

From the deck of Grandma's cabin, which must have been a hundred feet above the beach, I could see lights from Seattle across the water on a clear night. I used to imagine that maybe you could even see the tower on the old house where my bedroom was.

Once, before a visit to the island, I climbed to the top of the tower to see if I could see the cabin. All I saw was a glint of light off the metal roof of the ferry landing, and what seemed to be a few rooftops through the forested slopes above the beach. I knew exactly where the cabin was, but I couldn't see it. I didn't like that feeling.

"How could you know something is there but not see it?" I asked my mom.

"Life is like that."

"I don't know what you mean."

"Oh you do, I think."

"Maybe. Could you help a little?"

"Well it's like this. I can't see your dad, and Grandma can't see Grandpa, but I know they are with us when we think of them. Sometimes you just need to trust the way you feel, and believe what you think you know."

"Could you just...?"

"No, I will not risk my neck climbing that tower. I know the cabin is over there," and I knew the conversation was officially over.

CHAPTER 3

The Eagles

Grandma's beach cabin was actually invisible from the dirt road above. The only clue was a drift-wood plank nailed to the trunk of a dead fir tree. The treetop had broken off about twenty feet up, and had formed a guardrail along the downhill side of the dirt road. The sign said, "Eagle." This was their name. Below the sign, amid a dense growth of ferns much taller than I, and totally shaded by the evergreen canopy, began the trail to the cabin. The path tunneled through the blackberries and every so often sword ferns taller than a man. The trail hugged a giant cedar which seemed to anchor the slope and all of the lesser trees. Below the cedar, the hillside became steeper. The trail switched back and forth through a tangle of alders that defied gravity on the cliff.

Grandpa Eagle had built a deck across the front of the house from end to end. The deck had two levels, an outside fireplace, a flagpole, and a telescope. I watched the freighters as they became narrow slits of black creeping beyond the horizon.

Grandma could answer all my questions with stories about where the large cargo ships came from and where they were going. She would tell me about the lives of the fishermen who lived and worked on the smaller fishing boats. They worked nets out front in the fall, and fished in Alaska during spring and summer. Her stories would explain things, but most of all, the stories were really about people.

She used to say, "The only good things and bad things in this world are things which exist in the minds of people. Learn to find the good things and the bad things will never hurt you." When I asked her what she meant, she said, "Without people on this earth there would be nothing bad. Nature by itself is as God made it. So when you look at people, see the part that God put there. That will be the part that looks back at you and sends love and truth."

"Is it always that way?"

"Damn tootin'. Uh, I mean heck yes. The way I was taught, resentment doesn't come from God. People try to hide evil feelings in different ways because those feelings are unnatural. A person can't have resentment and honesty at the same time any more than the summer can be the winter." She had a knack for profound lessons, at least to the ears of an impressionable kid. They stuck with me though.

She used to call me the All American Kid, like she invented a superhero suit then cleaned me up and stuffed me into it. She told me often, "You are half white and half Indian so you have within you the power of both worlds, probably someday you will see the problems of both as well."

My reaction was, "Huh, half?" She did enough talking for two people and I sort of got used to just letting her run on. I liked the stories that seem to come out of nowhere. I hardly ever knew what to expect.

"Well, let's see. Your Great Grandpa was a Russian who married a beautiful Eskimo woman, so this makes me half. But your Grandpa was half Nez Perce and half Irish so I guess that makes your Mom Eskimo, Nez Perce, Russian, and Irish in equal parts. Your Dad was half Apache and half Scottish, so I guess it's just easier to say you're half Indian, though most Indian people would not forgive me for lumping them all together. The Irish, Scottish, and Russian sort of explains those deep green eyes of yours, though."

"Are they so different, the worlds I mean?"

The preacher was starting to come out again. "As time goes on they become more like one, and in eternity where we all shall reside one day, they are the same."

"If they are going to be the same, who cares?"

"Because there is a part inside of some people, a darkness that does not look back, and that darkness harbors resentment. You must learn to be aware of this."

"How can I tell?"

"It isn't that you should search for the dark spirit in people, but you must allow yourself to see when it is present. The old Indians say resentment is the spirit of evil. Knowing it is near is the best way to not let it have a home inside of you. "

"I don't want to."

"That is both the Indian way and the Christian way. Too bad people who hate are not aware."

"How do you know they aren't?"

Then the Indian in her took over. "Being truly aware of your feelings requires honesty. Hate and honesty can't live together in the same person. Old Chief Seattle would have said, 'It is as the sun cannot live with the stars.'" I had a feeling he had really said that a long time ago.

Grandma had explanations for everything. They were fun to listen to because she didn't know how to answer a question without telling a story. Because of all those visits to the beach cabin, and all those stories, we became friends long before she moved into the big house in Seattle.

I missed the trips to the cabin. They stopped when Grandpa died, and I missed him, too. I could hardly begin to imagine how much my grandma must have missed him. She knew him for almost fifty years. He was strong but thin, and because he was quiet, he was "hard to know," people said, and I agreed. He did not surround himself with friends, and seemed as though he preferred to be alone, a solitary eagle. Even when he was with people, his deep, black eyes seemed to focus far away. When there was music he changed. Suddenly he was like a movie star – charming and outgoing, for the moment anyway. He played the piano at the slightest hint of a request to do so, and he was good, darn good.

I realized one of those quiet days fishing with him, how hard it is to get to know someone, I mean really know them if they don't like to talk. There is no other way to know what they think and feel. Of course words can be just that, words, but I didn't think he would ever lie to me. I just wanted to know him.

What a difference there was between the two of them. They had shared fifty years of life together, but he was so quiet, I wondered if she felt like he wasn't there for some of it. I wondered if he was keeping something locked up inside of himself, something that belonged to everyone? I figured he could save anything he wanted, but I knew even then, the longer you save memories without sharing them the less valuable they become. I made a promise to myself one of those frustrating days that I would never hide from others, especially family.

I think Grandma knew too and perhaps she tried to make up for his silence. She was my most favorite person of all time, if such a distinction is possible. She knew everyone along the road to the cabin, and in the town. Along our beach walks, everyone we encountered knew her. On the beach they stopped her to talk or holler a hearty greeting from the cabins on the cliff. Smiles broke out and postures went to the over-the-back-fence, comfortable sort that friends use with each other. Whenever there was a crisis on the island, even the mayor and county officials were pulled to the cabin by the magnet of her personality and wisdom. In a lot of ways, she was the most unforgettable character of my life and the one I wanted most to be like. I remember her best when I sit quietly and read the poems she left behind at the house when she passed away. The poems are her story too.

CHAPTER 4

Broken Top

I'm no kid anymore and our Victorian mansion in the city is gone now, gobbled up by freeways, high rises, and thousands and thousands of people. The grand old trees that used to reach over the house are gone, and the narrow road that used to pass the huge Victorian on either side of the iron fence that ringed the grounds is now an expanse of concrete. You can't see Elliot Bay from there anymore because buildings tower around the property, and the turret of my bedroom, where the curved glass used to fend off the rain and capture the bay, is now buried by an office building.

Behind the house there was a stand of ancient firs where I used to play with my kid friends. Many times, we passed entire days there becoming Tarzan, Superman, The Green Hornet, The Shadow and other kid heroes. Wonder Woman and The Cat Lady were there too, and they worked their incredible feats of justice with the rest of us. On the Fourth of July we climbed the trees and watched fireworks in the city. One of the trees had its top snapped off in a lightning storm and the ragged top looked to us like a claw. Even without a top this giant was the tallest tree around. My friends and I liked to have our birthday parties in the tree house we had built in it, and called the tree Broken Top as if it had a first and last name.

Nobody knew how old Broken Top was or how it escaped the spree of logging that tackled the city ages before, when young Seattle was growing faster than the new settlement could tolerate. There was a time when trees represented a wilderness that was an enemy, an enemy civilized folks felt had to be tamed. From the early settlement on the shore of the bay, the hillsides around early Seattle looked like a sea of stumps.

Broken Top was more crooked than most evergreens, with a pronounced kink each third of the way to the missing crown. Perhaps the loggers, who did much of the work by hand, thought it would require too much sweat for a harvest of crooked logs when nearby brothers and sisters would fall predictably and lay as straight as their shadows on the forest floor. Broken Top was the only giant left standing on the hill.

Decades before, when the tree was much smaller, someone had scraped away the bark about a third of the way up, making a huge, smooth surface that stretched almost halfway around the tree. The scar had healed itself well, nearly closing off the cut entirely, but the culprit's handiwork was still visible. The bark had closed around the wound, ringing the smooth wood underneath to form a polished wood platter in the shape of a heart. Within the heart were two sets of initials, VB+SB June 1882, and below, SB+VB July 1885. 1882 is the year the old house was started; it said so on a stone set into the base of the front porch, which also noted the year of completion, 1885.

I loved the old tree, if it is possible to love a tree. The tree had been part of the wilderness before the city was there. It had lived in the forest when the Indians were custodians, before the invasion by whites. The bark was worn smooth by hands and feet of children, and it had lived and grown greater than any other tree on the hill. The branches were spaced for climbing, and the brown needles that blanketed the ground and choked out the grass were deep green and silver on the living tree. It was a place where I could live out my ten-year-old fantasies. It was a city, castle, mountain, ship, and kingdom, and it was alive.

Sometimes Broken Top was my theater, and the day I fell out of the tree, I was trying to show off to friends how I could climb down from a tree head first. My audience was the entire attendance of my tenth birthday party. In the midst of the wide-eyed group of faces, staring up at me in silence, was my best friend Bonnie, and her presence was the reason I felt I had to back up my bragging with a demonstration.

The tree house was equal in height to the third floor of the old mansion, so this wasn't just any tree house, but the best one on the entire hill, maybe even the entire city. Dad had built it out of lumber from some of the old houses that were being torn down to make way for a hospital not far away. I was about five or six years old when he hoisted the big pieces up the tree with an old ship's block and tackle, and I promised to cut the grass forever if he would leave the pulley in the tree with the rope coming through the floor as our elevator.

"I promise, I promise."

"Seems to me you are making a promise you can't even keep yet. I doubt you can even push the mower."

"I'm getting real strong. Big, too."

"Sure but do you realize how long forever is? Forever is longer than the tree or the tree house will even be here. That is also longer than you and I will be here."

I had to think about it for a while. Somehow he had made my generous offer rather impossible. I was about to offer something else when he started to build a proper ladder up the tree starting about fifteen feet above the ground, and told me when I was big enough to climb to the first rung, the tree house would be mine, pulley and all. The first rung was a long way up and the tree didn't have any branches low enough for me to reach, so I guess he thought I was grounded for a few years. When he was done, it didn't take me long to gather a hammer, nails, and pieces of wood, and nail cross pieces to the tree so I could climb to his first rung. My part wasn't much of a ladder, and I didn't get finished. When he saw my attempt, he built a proper one from the ground up.

He climbed the ladder partway up and made a mark on the tree beyond which I was forbidden to pass without permission.

Each week or so the mark got raised, and soon just my own fear kept me in the lower branches.

Four years later, it was through the floor of the tree house, down the so-called "elevator" that I fell head first. This couldn't really be called an accident, though, as Grandma and the neighbors soon found out. The word got out I was putting on a demonstration for my friends – showing off, actually. At the time I thought it was a demonstration of bravery, but the popular vote later said it was a demonstration of stupidity. I was showing everyone how it was possible to come down from the tree head first. Not even cats, raccoons, or birds came down head first.

I had a good grip on the rope for the first few feet, then the fat hemp hawser which had been worn smooth by too many children's hands and too many years of use on the busy decks of too many ships, started to slip through my grip. I clamped down harder but the rope still moved, slowly at first, then faster, and faster, feeling suddenly hot against my wet palms. I had prepared for this possibility by wearing my mother's woolen winter mittens, though it was mid-summer. Something went wrong with my plan, though, because I couldn't stop myself, and the world in front of me began to travel with the quickened rhythm of my heart. I was building up speed like a diving fighter plane and a runaway locomotive all rolled into one. The rope whizzed and smoked, burned through my mittens and hummed through my thighs making the sound of a zipper against the legs of my jeans where I had them clenched around the rope. Falling with unchecked speed, the rough trunk of the old tree blurred past by my face so fast I couldn't tell where I was. I held on until I hit the roots, grass, and needle-covered rocks at the bottom of the elevator. I remember thinking, "I'm falling head first and there is nothing I can do about it. This is going to be really bad, really bad." A character-giving scar on my forehead still bears the evidence of a sudden stop, some fifty-five years later.

It was Grandma who gathered me up off the ground that

day among the screaming kids, who ran around the neighborhood to tell everyone Hecky was dead.

"Hecky's dead, Hecky's dead!"

"He fell off the tree house."

"Nu-uh, he dove off."

"Didn't either, he dove off the house."

"Didn't either."

"Did to."

"He broke his arms and legs, trying to fly off the roof. I saw him."

"He almost flew, too."

"No. He fell straight down like a train. He didn't move. He bled a lot, and now he's dead."

So by the time Grandma got there other people were starting to show up to see the body. Grandma stopped some of the bleeding and pulled my teeth out of my lip, then she put me into my wagon and pulled me down the street and around the corner to the doctor. He was an obstetrician but he made short work of sewing me up and setting my broken arm and dislocated shoulder – at least this is what I am told, for I remember very little. I was carried back to the old house and put to bed knowing from then on, this was going to be a long and slow summer.

The good weather was just coming to Seattle after having waited somewhere else for the winter rains to leave. The outdoors was fresh and green with all the flowers in their spring colors, and birds were beginning to nest in the trees out back and under the eaves. My friends and I had made plans for the summer, but for me there would be no swimming or bikes, no tree climbing or baseball, no adventures or exploring, just books, and Grandma. In my misery she would say, "Everything will be okay, for you have within you all of the strength of the oceans and the tide. Your family has been born upon the tide and wind, and you will be fine because you are as strong as the tide, and the ocean behind it." I didn't know what this meant, and actually I had a hard time thinking of anything except how badly I hurt all over. I just remembered how strange a thing it was to say to a kid who had just fallen out of a tree, especially when it was his own fault.

The next morning my arm ached, and I could not talk because my mouth was so swollen. I eased myself out of bed, feeling like the lawnmower I had once left out in the rain, and whose rusted wheels now refused to move. Cutting the lawn had been the furthest thing from my mind all spring, but for some reason, I now felt guilty for ruining the mower. I decided to store the mower inside as soon as I was able to move it.

As I eased my aching self out of the covers and onto the edge of the bed, I doubted I would be able to stand. I staggered to my feet like the old people in my dream, and lumbered across the linoleum that surrounded my bed. I felt hot and dizzy so I leaned against the window frame. I pushed the bandages to my forehead, away from my eyes, and tried to look out the turret window. I wanted to see the ferries and fishing boats, but the early morning rain beat on the curved glass, blurring everything – and besides I could barely see out of my swollen eyelids.

My senses were awake enough to detect the pop and smell of kindling starting the coal fire in the kitchen cook stove. The black monster crackled and popped as Grandma rattled the grate and shoveled a load of coal into the open mouth. She liked to do this on chilly mornings instead of turning the furnace on because she said it reminded her of her own mother and the times they had together in this house. She didn't want Mom to buy a new stove and said she would do all of the cooking if we kept the old one. I always thought she would have done it all anyway, but we kept the thing for her and it made the kitchen look like a blacksmith shop. Grandma was content to spend hours cooking for anyone who needed food. Her recipes were always slightly different and always better than anyone else's. Said she "played the range and cooked by ear."

If friends were down on their luck she was the first one there with a meal. When things were really bad total strangers were treated like family. She regularly took hot food to the Sailor's Mission on the waterfront at the base of the long hill. Old sailors lived there – or, "Made their last port," as she would say. I think the Mission and the sailors were on her mind a lot more than she let on. To know Grandma you had to understand the way she felt about that place.

The Mission was built on a pier that crawled out over the water as an extension of a dry land warehouse. In those days, the Seattle waterfront was a series of piers jutting out into Elliot Bay. Ships would tie up alongside them and the longshoremen transferred the cargo using the warehouse space until trucks and trains could move it all again. There was always plenty of activity to watch as the ships came and went. Cargo booms swung loads of goods out of train cars stationed on the dock and into the cavernous hulls. Shipping operations were underway twenty-four hours a day every day of the year, rain or shine. The equipment shook the wooden piers and rattled the old warehouse windows and planks. Forklifts carrying pallets of goods were shunted to just the right place by gangs of men with white caps, black pants, suspenders, and union buttons. Worker bees taking care of the hive.

The Mission was on the top floor of one of the old warehouse piers – a sort of attic cobbled together between the roof and the crossbeams. The space was one of those emergency work areas created during the war effort then abandoned and forgotten. Since it was an afterthought and hurriedly done, not enough attention had been paid to making a safe and easy way in and out. Access was by rickety stairs connected to a catwalk at the deep-water end of the warehouse. The catwalk crossed under the roof beams about thirty feet above the warehouse floor then climbed to a set of double doors that closed in four-fifths of the pier's upper floor. The double doors slid sideways to reveal a cavernous room with windows clouded with soot, dust and bird poop all around. It was a huge room, like a gymnasium or even bigger, with lots of unpainted timbers going straight up to the roof itself. Bones holding the building together.

I went there with my kid friends once. We used to call it The Mission Pier. Outside, there was a ship from Alaska. Pallets of canned salmon were being unloaded using long booms controlled by a maze of cables and winches. Men were on the ship and on the dock. Carts and forklifts shuttled back and forth into the bottom floor of the warehouse. There was a lot of shouting, signal whistles, and machinery noises. Later, other men and machines arrived at the bottom floor of the warehouse, where trucks hauled away the crates. The Seattle waterfront was alive in those days. It was the heart of the city, pumping goods in and out.

Upstairs, inside the gymnasium-like room, there were four rows of iron cots. They reminded me of pictures I had seen of an army barracks, or of prison camps, except nothing was painted and all of the blankets were worn and of different colors. Some of the cots did not have pillows. A few of them were occupied by old men who seemed to be awake but just looking at the walls. One of them stirred and rolled his head to squint at us in the half-light, eyes watering.

"Hey lads," he said, and waved a bare forearm dark with tattoos. He reached beneath the cot for a dark green bottle. "Ship's in the bottle now," waving it feebly.

"You have a ship in a bottle?"

"Ay, but what good is that? This other has the medicine. Cure your ills, straighten your hair, remove paint." He had a second bottle in his other hand. "Well, fellas, when you get like this, the whole world is in a bottle. Can't stand a watch, can't mend a sail. Been too many years on the sea, but I'd do anything to be there again. Just can't get this old body to work right any more. Don't matter too much, though, cause there ain't no sailing ships anymore, anyways."

"Have you been around the world?"

"Mates I have been to hell and back." He coughed and his face turned red. He steadied himself on an elbow, spilling a drop, and went on. "The things I have seen and done will get me there again soon enough. Yes, I have been around the world. I have sailed where the winds took me, and I left my heart spread in the wake of ships. I have known brave men and cowards, princes and whores. I have known love and hate but now that I am wise enough to know only love counts, it is too damned late for me." He coughed again and wiped his eyes with a sleeve. "Sail the clear water ahead, mates. Steer clear of the reefs. Weather the storms." He began to gasp and cough again. "The thing for you to remember, lads, is that life without risk is not life. Life without risk is not worth living."

He started coughing, drained the bottle, then dropped it onto the floor. His head fell back onto the stained faded grey and yellow pillow. As he waved us away, we could see through his open collar that his body was covered with tattoos. One hand clutched the green bottle with a ship inside.

Some mattresses were piled in a corner, and an old, one-eyed cat sat atop the pile, staring at a hole in the floor. The room smelled of tobacco and wet wool. There were water stains on the floor where the tin roof had leaked. There were four stoves in the room, all of them made from old oil drums. Along the walls hung old newspaper photos and magazine cut-outs with pictures of ships. Over the double door someone had nailed a sign carved out of wood, it read, DISCOVERY, and appeared to be very old.

When Grandma visited the old men here, I know she felt a genuine sorrow for them. She said, "My sadness is because they have lived on the sea and now the wind and tide takes them no further. They long to be on the swells of the great ocean, and they dream of the sailing ships which are all gone. Among themselves they talk of the places they have seen and the things they have done, but the grandest experiences they share are the stories of storms at sea, and how the fury of nature makes a man look into his own soul. None of these men have anything, or want anything. Now they are put aside like a broken and rotted hull. They will not feel the sea under them again, they will not see another sunset or sunrise on a pitching deck. They know they will die, land-bound, just as sure as if each of them were anchored here in the mud. When they were young, they chose the sea as a way of life. Now it has cast them ashore, broken and lonely, and I am saddened by that. But their fondest memories are of the sea and somehow the sea still gives them the strength to go on."

Sometimes she would come back from the Mission looking very tired, and sit for a long time in front of the stove with her hands in her lap. Sometimes she cradled a green bottle with a beautiful ship inside. The detail was incredible. With a magnifying glass you could see the ship's name – *Discovery.*

CHAPTER 5

Castaways

Humankind in far off places,
Squinting toward the distant shore.
Knowing of the ghostly faces,
And feeling the empty space inside.
Does one mourn the loss of others more,
Or commit oneself to the ebbing tide?

I felt that she might have been sitting there for a long time before I came in. The green bottle was in her apron pocket as she leaned forward in the chair and said, "Better do your best to get comfortable if you can. You tell me if I go on too long or if you need anything. Are you ready?" Then she paused and stood for a moment, looking beyond the space in front of her, sort of like she was listening to something I couldn't hear, her memories maybe. Next she walked to the stove, and again opened it, rattled the grate and threw into the fire three more shovels of coal. The fire began to burn brighter and higher through the open door the way I liked best. She closed the door and we could see the white flames lick at the hinges and cracks around the edges. Warmth reached me where I sat at the table across the room. She sat again, nestled into her chair, and started in her low strong voice. Sweet and gentle, the cello. Comforting, confident and caring. She chose her words carefully, almost as if she was reading a book.

"In Alaska, far north of the Arctic Circle, it was early springtime. The sea around the finger of land where this story starts was not quite so black and angry as it had been days before. Even so, the wind gusts and dangerous seas were still building far out on the ocean and driving huge waves against the shore. The sea and the storms were such familiar things on this Arctic shore that they were accepted like the air itself. They were part of life like a shadow is a part of life.

"The sandy shore and scattered pebbles accepted the ocean's fury with a familiarity born from thousands of years serving as buffer between creatures of the land and creatures of the sea. The shore muffled and quieted the breakers. The beach formed itself into a ramp of polished, sparkling pebbles pushing up from the ocean into rolling plains covered with coarse grasses and willows. The matted ground between the willows showed traces of snow and patches of ice. There were no trees and no color.

"Away from the beach, a network of paths wore through the surface growth. Like a web, they led to a large circle where nothing grew. Within the edge of the circle stood a handful of small huts. Their shapes were rough and uneven. They were low in their profile because they were built partly below the ground. The exteriors were covered in sod knit together with an assortment of driftwood and animal bones.

"The small village was quiet with no signs of people or animals. Just above the line of the beach, beyond the first small hillocks of bunched grasses, more of the paths led in various directions.

"Everyone in the village had known the sea, its ice, and its storms. The villagers had been there longer than anyone could remember, and they depended on the nearby sea for everything. These people lived by the sea, and sometimes died by the sea. In this primitive time and harsh place, a hundred or so years ago, those who fished beyond the sight of shore or ventured far out onto the ice when the seasons were turning, protected themselves with chants and tokens. They made many promises not knowing if the sea would return them safely or forever take them away. In this place I am telling you about, as strange as this may seem, there once were many more women and small children than there were men, and thus it had always been. This village was the only home my mother had known as a child, but she had to leave it.

"Imagine her if you can as a young girl, her feet leaving a trail in the sand away from this village, her footprints disappearing behind her. Imagine the wind blowing in gusts off the sea and its chill coming with a hollow whistle that took away her breath. She lowered her face into the loose folds of clothing under her chin. The sod and driftwood huts of the village she had left were now two full days behind her. She left behind everyone and everything, and she thought she would not see that place again. She carried with her only things she would need to survive on this journey south, but she did not know how long it would take or where it would end.

"By late afternoon her steady walking through the storm had taken her far beyond the cape where the villagers foraged in the summer among the low bushes and bogs. She had never been this far from the village before, and did not know how much farther she would need to go. As she watched the seabirds being blasted by the gusts across the waves, and hang motionless in the wind, she wondered how they stayed alive when ice covered all of the sea.

"She moved on and would travel until daylight faded. A mad wind beat the shore without mercy, carrying salt spray well into the beach line, and it ran in rivulets under her clothes. The sand gave way to scattered stones, and the shore no longer faded landward gently – there was now a steep bluff that hemmed the beach and kept her closer to the water and the wind borne spray. The scattered stones soon became an expanse of pebbles, and the bluff grew higher and steeper. She hoped she would not be caught without an escape when the tide came in. The sandy bluff revealed outcrops of rocks, and soon the pebbles of the beach turned into large broken boulders each one an island. She needed to climb and jump from place to place as the incoming tide continued to force her against the boulders above the tide pools. The combination of an incoming tide, storm driven waves, and the steepness of the shore caused the waves to break ever closer to the headwall. Once in a while an especially large breaker would send her scampering up the rocks at the base of the cliff, where they were slippery with green algae, too far above the normal tide to grow the rough, foot-catching colonies of barnacles.

"It would be dark again soon. She was tired; and for every sharp, steep outcropping of rock she surmounted, another, awaited her around every bend of the shoreline. Her clothes heavy with sea spray, she stopped for a short rest, and in moments felt as if the cold sea was running into the cuffs and seams. She felt the comfort, though, in the smells of home and family in the loose folds around her shoulders. Knowing she had to force herself onward to stay warm, she rose quickly and pushed on, balancing herself against each gust of wind.

"She could not go back. Days before, a sickness came to the village and the fever had taken almost everyone quickly. This took place in a time when there were no airplanes, telephones, automobiles, miracle drugs, radios or any of the other modern inventions we have now come to rely on. There was no way to slow the sickness, or stop it, or rescue people from it. For some reason, she was the only one who had not become ill. She was the only one left alive.

"In the village, the winter had been worse than any before it, and the food gathered and preserved from the previous summer harvest season did not last to the late thaw. Game had been difficult to find late the previous summer, and throughout the fall.

"Late in the fall, as the sea froze over, all of the men from the village went to hunt seals far out on the ice. Far offshore, they pulled their kayaks onto the ice and began their patient wait at the breathing holes. Then the ice separated, leaving an open lead between the hunters and the shore, and another open lead between them and their kayaks. They had no choice but to wait on the drifting ice island hoping for the gap to close. On the second day of waiting, the floating island split then became unbalanced. The half on which nobody was standing overturned and sent a wave that overturned the other half. All of the men were swept into the sea. None of them survived

"In deep winter, there were many wolves and they pushed the caribou herds far beyond the distant hills many days travel from the village. This exceeded the range, ability, and survival skills of the village boys. The wolves were bold around the village, taking some food stores and challenging the village dogs. The strongest dogs defended against the pack while the weaker ones cowered and whined. The wolves killed the strongest dogs and left the weaker ones alone.

"The village was without men when the fever struck. The fever sickness came suddenly, and within two days everyone was ill. Three days later most had died. The tiny village had more bad luck in one year than ten villages should have in a hundred years.

"The deep tiredness of cold and loneliness dragged at her legs as the late afternoon cast its long shadows across the earth. From her place on the beach, she watched the grasses on the bluff above her as they performed their drunken dances in the wind. She felt as if their shadows reached out to enfold her. The sound and smell of the land and sea were all around her, but these things she knew best would not dispel her loneliness, for her dearest friends, her family, and everyone she had known were all dead.

"She forced herself to continue through the sloping field of sea boulders. Everything about the shore became meaner and she found it difficult to walk between the head high boulders but they were becoming too rounded, slippery, and high to jump from rock to rock. Shaven heads with no shoulders she thought. When she tried to climb one she slipped off its neck into a shallow pool of seawater, getting soaked to the thighs, twisting an ankle.

"She decided she had to climb away from the beach before the incoming tide trapped her in the seaweed tangles and chasms of the boulder field. Heading toward the bluff and away from the sea, in a few minutes the line she chose seemed to end against a steep rock cliff. She studied the rock face leading to the top, looking for ledges and hand holds. She wished the slick algae and moss did not extend so far but it covered nearly every surface of the blocky ancient black as she worked her way onward and upward. Arriving at a vantage point high on the cliff, she could see the boulder field faded again to scattered stones and pebbles less than a quarter mile away. Changing her mind about climbing the rest of the way to the top, she decided she needed to pick her way across the near vertical headwall parallel to the water. It looked like she could gradually descend the hundred feet or so during the crossing and be back on the beach where the walking would be easier.

"Too stubborn to go back or to find a place to wait out the incoming tide, she flattened herself against the cliff face and reached out, carefully putting one hand into a crack. Then she moved a foot, rubbing it across the precipice until she felt a tiny outcropping. Crossing the face and descending at the same time, she moved the other foot, then a hand. Inch by inch, she moved across and downward on the steepest part, gaining confidence, but as she moved a foot onto the next ledge, a tightening feeling within told her the ridge was too small, too slippery, too sloped – and as a roaring gust blasted across the sea cliff and tore at her garments, she began to lose her balance. She grabbed at the glossy black surface, moss, wetness, cold, slipping past her cheek, her fingernails scratching, and sliding as if on ice. The sky, wind, and sea began to spin as she plummeted into darkness, clawing at the air and tumbling away from the dark rocks in a silent fall to a tangled mound of seaweed on the beach thirty feet below.

"This same storm which made it so difficult for her to make her way across the cliff had also caused a great deal of discomfort aboard a whaling vessel called the *Beluga*, which at the moment of her fall was standing at anchor in thirty fathoms in a fog bank less than a mile offshore and less than three miles from where the girl had stopped to rest that afternoon. At this exact spot where her body now lay on the beach, the *Beluga* had put ashore a three-man hunting party three days before.

"Native Americans lived along the Arctic coast of North America long before recorded history. In the 1800s, when this story happened, trappers and explorers from other cultures began to visit these native lands. In the waters of the North Pacific, white men became used to venturing across great distances and surviving many weeks at sea in search of whales, otters, foxes, and mink, all available for nothing more than the trouble to take them. Voyages aboard whaling vessels were long, and the conditions on the older sailing ships were trying. Food rations were frequently cold, sometimes moldy, and the unheated quarters cramped and wet.

"In those days, captains seized opportunities to send hunting parties ashore to replenish water and food supplies. Even well equipped vessels like the 200-ton, square rigged brigantine, *Beluga*, made a practice of sending small hunting parties ashore to help vary the diets of the men living on the ship. Food was easy to get from the sea, but deer, moose, and caribou boosted crew morale.

"Because of the storm, the *Beluga's* hunting party was stranded on shore. The storm, which had been a factor in the girl falling from the cliff, was also keeping the three men from launching their longboat into the building surf. They had no choice but to wait out their third night ashore. Despite success of the hunt, the extended shore visit was becoming uncomfortable. There were no trees in this place, and it was difficult for them to fashion a warm, dry shelter with just tundra, brush, driftwood, and grass. But, the grasses were tough and reedy enough to thatch over the jumbled driftwood frame, and the men fashioned together a coarse lean-to. In silent agreement, driven by their instincts, they erected a tiny shelter out of reach of the waves under a grass thatched earthen overhang, which centuries of rain and snow melt had cut into the cliff high above the beach. They had four caribou pelts from a fresh kill to help keep them warm, and a small canvas to help keep out the rain.

"They needed to wait out the weather until sea conditions improved enough to make travel back to the *Beluga* possible in the small open boat. A glimmer of hope arose when the sky had cleared the night before, but the wind continued to howl and the swells became taller and steeper with the driving wind. Farther seaward, in the deep water between the shore and the *Beluga,* the waves were so steep and tall that the crests were breaking off and falling into the dark troughs between them. Every breaker shooting into the beach was a seething black mountain that could bury the boat in its curl.

"The frigid wind from off shore was coming from the cooling effect of the winter pack ice which should have been gone by now. Formed during winter in the open ocean, in the spring the pack fractured and drifted apart becoming small ice drifts with large expanses of open water with the spring breakup. Having already broken apart, the small separate bergs were being fused together again by winds and currents and the growing field was being driven toward the shore in a jumbled, grinding mass. The watch on the *Beluga* must have become aware of the ice field at first light, though like the Grim Reaper, the ice had been silently closing in on them since nightfall of the previous day. Only a mile offshore, the shore party did not hear the *Beluga's* evening concertina music and singing that often filled the air when the ship was at anchor. From the shore they had not seen any lights from the oil lamps the crew used below decks. The fog sealed off the sound and the light, as if everyone aboard retired with the falling darkness. Still, though, it was unimaginable to think there would not have been at least an alert anchor watch.

"Just before dawn from the hilltop vantage point looking out to sea from just above the shelter, the leader of the shore party noticed a far-off reflection of brightness on the horizon. Without a second look, panic and terror surged through him. Death was creeping in to trap and crush them, pack ice. The ice field itself was not visible in the pre dawn but the even shade of whiteness on the horizon suggested it was there, already packed tight and was being driven landward by the inshore wind and near-shore current. Perhaps the storm and the fog, now gone at first light, had obscured it from the *Beluga's* lookout until now or maybe it had moved in rapidly during the night. The whiteness seemed to extend across the entire horizon, locking out all paths to freedom. Even in the early dawn light he was certain of what this was, and he knew the hunting party must leave immediately to rejoin the *Beluga*. He was certain the *Beluga* would not risk being caught in the ice, and the captain would undoubtedly leave as soon as they made out the ice-trap creeping in on them. He knew the captain would abandon the three-man shore party to save the *Beluga* from being crushed.

"Onboard the *Beluga*, the night watch had taken his place near the forepeak the previous evening, and spent his time worrying about the ship dragging anchor as the wind had been gusting from offshore for an entire day, and the tackle strained with each heaving, surging whack of each swell. Untiring, the grey walls charged at the pace of running horses over and over through the night and still the watch did not look out to sea. He was trying to keep warm tucked into a canvas letting the spray splash from his back. Wet wool cap pulled down to his nose, and fingers clamping closed the canvas scrap, he curled in the shelter of the bow and did not raise himself above the rail except to judge the distance from shore and take soundings during the night. He yelled the soundings back to the wheel watch and they varied little through the night.

"'Hail the watch. Man in chains says by the mark three.

By the mark three," waiting for the answer back.

"'By the mark three," and another hour would go by.

"After a day of wind and rain, the night air had gotten colder by the hour, and a flurry of snow kicked in front of the blasts of frigid air penetrating the lean-to. In spite of the party's hunting success they were now thoroughly drenched, in low spirits, tired, and cold. They had built a small driftwood fire and kept it burning through the night. They had hoped for the weather to calm and allow them to launch the boat into the surf at first light, but when the dawn came with clear sky, the wind continued to churn the sea into earth shuddering breakers of terrifying height. All three men were excellent seamen – good enough to recognize that the mountainous seas made their chances of survival through the lines of breakers slim. They would get only one chance.

"For his part, the *Beluga's* captain knew the possibility of ice when he dropped anchor and sent the party ashore. He was a wise and experienced man and weighed the remoteness of the risk against the potential consequences. Some ice could blow in he thought, but at this time of year the pack could never trap them solid. There wasn't enough floating ice to lock them in and the *Beluga* was not at risk. At worst, he thought a few ice flows might slow their travel but could not trap them, drive them ashore, or crush the hull.

"He had not taken into account that the *Beluga* might not be able to escape under sail. Now there was little that could be done, for the *Beluga* with her square rigging could not point high enough into the wind to make an offshore tack. The combination of headwind, incoming tide and blocking ice flow meant pulling anchor would commit the ship to be tossed ashore. The captain had to wait for at least a twenty degree shift of the wind, and probably a cycle of the tide, then attempt to get underway even if the sea did not calm. The shore party would have to fend for themselves until the *Beluga* could return to the anchorage, if the captain chose to risk a return.

"Back on the bluff, the shore party was more willing to risk action than the crew and officers aboard the *Beluga*. In their minds they had to reach the ship at all costs because there was a chance the *Beluga* might not return for them. They rushed into it. The night sky had not yet given way to the dawn as the three men started to drag the heavy kegs, and carcasses to the beach and began to load the longboat. They tied the water casks together and placed them at center of the boat, and wedged them against the garboards so they would not come loose. The four caribou carcasses were tied together and wedged against the casks. They left the hides behind in the shelter to make room for the meat. If the boat were to capsize, perhaps they would be able to right it again after its cargo fell into the sea, so they tied nothing down.

"They were almost reckless in their haste to get underway. They had tied the boat well above high tide and now that the tide was out they had to drag the loaded boat a quarter mile to the water. They were heaving with exhaustion when they reached the cold waters of the Chukchi Sea. With the rising sun, the wind shifted coming less from offshore. Now the breakers were becoming smaller but the wind gusts were still strong enough to blow the tops off the waves and give the sea a smoky look. The captain aboard the *Beluga* breathed a sigh of relief.

"The shore party strained to launch the longboat in the confusion of shifting wind, breakers, and a tide rip. At the same moment, the crew on the *Beluga* raised its jib and began to haul the mainsail. The stubby ship's old-fashioned square rig required wind from behind, but now it seemed the best the crew could hope for was getting nearly broadside to the wind with a push from the tide. The captain sensed there was a shift in the air. He prayed this would take them offshore and possibly allow them to skirt the ice pack. They fired a round from the deck cannon to alert the shore party, and raised the signal flags to make their intentions clear. They saw the panic on the shore, but did not wait.

"The shore party was taking the first pull on the oars when

the cannon fired. The blast went unheard in the roar of the surf. The boat continued into the water; two, three, four, five pulls on the oars. One man pulled and the other two lay in the bottom to keep the boat's center of gravity low.

"A colt of a wave came from the side and splashed against the gunwale, rolling the boat dangerously and shifting the weight of the animal carcasses. One oar dipped deep into the water. The oarsman was not quick at getting it free and the boat heeled further to that side, but righted itself as the oar came clear. Short hard pulls moved the boat into the first breaker line. The open boat stood on its stern, then the bow plunged into the darkness of the trough. Now there was nothing to be seen ahead but the great grey hill of water hissing, halfway to the sky. Behind it still a greater mountain, racing faster still, green and curling, head torn away by the wind. Almost no water came aboard in the first line of breakers now behind them, between them and the shore. There could be no turning back.

"'It was a big green one, mates,' hollered the oarsman above the roar of the sea. 'Grip her hard, mates, we're in for a growler. They're hissing and shooting. They're breaking out to sea beyond the shallows.'

"'Can you see the *Beluga*, can you steer to her?' hollered the smallest man from the bilge, where he lay flat with his arms stretched across the beam as if on a crucifix.

"Only the oarsman could see the next wave. It hid the small boat in the shadow of its curl, then lifting it spinning to the height of the roller, it boiled them deep into its teeth, the wind, the sea, the forces of nature clenching them down, binding and biting them with its thunder. The crushing wave drove everything backwards, and the oarsman's seat shattered. Oak barrels hammered their way trough the stern. The boat opened like a broken clamshell and the tangle of water casks, animal carcasses, and one lifeless human body slid through the gaping stern. The splintered boat rolled with lightening speed and shot beneath the sea.

"Two of the three men survived, exhausted and shivering, swept back to the beach by the battering sea. Barely conscious and shivering uncontrollably, one dragged the other back to the shelter. The smaller survivor was badly hurt. They had lost firearms and powder when the boat rolled, and in the force of the wave that propelled them to shore, coats and shoes had been ripped off. The stronger one was able to nurse the fire back to life. He covered them both in the caribou hides they had left behind in the shelter. If the weather did not warm soon, survival would be difficult and maybe impossible for the two of them.

"With supplies gone, the stronger man, the one called Baronoffsky, the ship's carpenter, ventured to the bluff throughout the day to see if the storm had returned any of their wreckage to the beach. The fog came in and masked the beach but each time he climbed down to walk the strand he was able to reclaim something pushed in on the tide. At midday, from the bluff, the ribbon of fog along the beach unwrapped then closed in again. He saw something moving toward them, just a speck in the far distance too far off for him to be sure what it was. His shout and wave vanished into the returning fog. He watched again later that afternoon as the fog was replaced by the low clouds and driving rain. The figure came into view again this time heading toward the cliff then disappearing in the boulder fields. He could see it was a person.

CHAPTER 6

The Shore

The men in the shore party were much like the rest of the crew of the *Beluga*, sinewy, raw-boned men, strong from years of bracing themselves against the motion of the ship. Their diet of salt meat, fish and bread kept them lean, if not healthy. On longer voyages many of them became ill, and even the healthiest of them faced high risk of injury on a sailing ship. On a voyage like this a season before, the *Beluga* had lost four experienced sailors and hunters to the sea.

"The ship was home to the crew, and the crew was a family to the men aboard, but like any sailing ship the *Beluga* could be a dangerous place. Wooden ships are never quiet. Their timbers work against blocks and sheets, and the sound of the sea itself comes through the hull. The *Beluga* was strongly built and the crew kept her well, though even the *Beluga* dealt out its share of sickness, scrapes, bruises, and cuts. With no ship's doctor on this or any other trading company vessel, men with serious injuries depended on anyone willing to help.

"All of the vessels had a carpenter to make casks, mend rigging, and repair the longboats and dories. Most of the carpenters became quite experienced at fashioning splints for broken limbs. Even so, a broken bone often meant a long, painful injury aggravated by the ship's motion, lack of medicines, and the presence of 'cures' worse than the injury itself. Nevertheless the ship's carpenter was an honored and respected man, held in high esteem among the ship's officers.

"In this story I am telling you, we shall call the leader of the shore party the carpenter, for when he signed on for an adventure at sea, that is the job he was hired for. He had a powerful body, and deep set blue eyes seeming to pierce everything they saw. A thick neck and strong torso made his motions appear blocky, though they could be startlingly quick and fluid. The carpenter and all others aboard the ship had hands like leather. Cables, winches, lines, sails, and tools hardened their palms and built strong arms, shoulders, and backs. Men were the engine that allowed the wind to drive the ship.

"The captain of the *Beluga* knew this man was not exactly just another ship's carpenter, though no one spoke about his past. It had become clear to the captain that this particular carpenter was an educated man, for he had saved them a year before when a storm did serious damage to the bridge deck and washed the ship's charts, sextant, and copy of the Bowdich overboard. Among all of the ship's officers and crew, only the carpenter was able to star sight and calculate a course safely home. During that same event, the *Beluga* came within shouting distance of a Russian vessel, and the carpenter was able to talk with them and trade tobacco, bread and rum. This was especially startling, because much of the trading was done in French and Spanish.

"International crews were common aboard sailing vessels. Tasks that required brawn were not complex. They had to be done correctly and at the right time, but did not require a great deal of speaking to be accomplished. Since communication of simple tasks could be done in simple terms, few officers learned any language but their own. So the officers of the *Beluga* had a new respect for, if not suspicion of, the carpenter, for they knew he also spoke Russian and English.

"Shipmates in the crew quarters shared a close life in a dark, unheated, half height space, which for some reason or another was called the forecastle. Life was a wet, stooped existence more suited to a dungeon than a castle. The cramped quarters offered a warren of closely packed wooden slabs built as part of the hull tight against the outside curve of the oak. Each bunk had a straw mattress and a small fishnet hammock in which all personal belongings were stored. There were no secret places, no drawers or cabinets, no privacy. At one end sat a shared slop bucket and at the other a water barrel with a single shared drinking cup hung from it. The crew shared watches around the clock and those who ate together would stand watch together. Hours often passed in silence, but even so in such circumstances it is possible to know a person by their actions as much as by their words.

"Hecky, now I am going to tell you about something which happened nearly a year before, when the *Beluga* had come upon a pod of whales in a near dead calm. This will help you know a bit more about this character we are calling the ship's carpenter. This was a rare day, for the sea was flat in a way it hardly ever is. The air was warm, the sun bright, and you could see deeply into the glassy water. There was no sound but the hushed flapping of loose lines and canvas, and then the abrupt whoosh and sigh of whales nearby awakened and alarmed all hands. Barnacle covered backs rose and pushed through the water, with a great sigh, the whales surfaced close alongside the *Beluga,* then dove again in a rhythm they would keep up for thousands of miles north.

"It is more properly said, the whales came upon the *Beluga*, rather than the other way around. Her mizzen was slapping against the sidestays and the boom rattling loosely when the whales were sighted. The boat had taken on a comfortable beam end roll, and the rhythm matched the soft creak of its timbers and the slow working of canvas and rope in wooden blocks. Everything said this was a time for napping on deck in the sun. It was early spring and the *Beluga* was in southern waters, so the sun against the cabin passageway trapped heat and warmed the sailors' backs. The cry of 'Whale Ho!' came far later than it should have.

"There was a scramble to put boats over the side, and though this had been done many times before, the calm of the sea would take the lives of John Moresby, Eathan Willis, Gilbert Olander, and the big black man called Adam, who had shackle scars around his wrists and ankles, and terrible lash marks across his broad back, but whose real name no one knew.

"The accident happened as the crew scrambled to lower the boats. A block fowled, a davit broke, a line parted, and the boat and its crew fell into the icy sea, stern first. Lines tangled around the men, and when they surfaced, they were being slowly trolled behind the ship. The tangle of block, davit, and hemp wound itself around the torso of each man, and became snarled underwater against the rudder. The men struggled to work themselves free, but two were dragged under. A clutch of sickened men at the rail of the boat deck watched them sink under the slick window of the near-calm wake. Wide eyed, open mouthed terror looked back. The struggle slowed for two of them and their faces, barely beneath the crystal clear water, turned pale and gray.

"As the crew swiftly put another boat over the side, the sharks came. The remaining two men still hopelessly knotted and choking for air, worked feebly to free themselves as the sharks closed in. In the screaming, the water thrashed and went red, and in moments, the air was quiet and the sharks were gone. The *Beluga* sailed on in the near calm, leaving behind a pinkness in its wake.

"Hecky, you need to realize, in those days, no one had hopes of getting rich from the sea except those who financed the ships and conducted the trade. Ship's officers shared in the bounty, and were not bashful about recounting their heroics to assure the owners of their loyalty and indispensability. Those who were the muscle and heart of the ship could keep a family ashore, but life was hard for them, and their low place in society was certain because it resulted from a sailor's meager income. Two incomes made things easier so families sent more sons to sea by the generation, and the fleet never fell short of crew. As sure as the passing of the seasons, there were memorial funerals with no bodies to bury, and it seemed the number of young men and boys claimed by the sea always exceeded the number of old men left to sit on porches, facing the sea. There were few old men, and many widows.

"When the *Beluga* returned to port after the disaster, the bad news was circulating in town before the ship was in the harbor. Widows who had grieved before and who had shared tales of lost sons and lovers stood in a dark cluster on the dock even before the *Beluga* was made fast to the moorage. The somber crowd seemed to hold the women up and surround them in a shroud of sadness. There were no children present. Three old men stood together in the drizzle at the landward end of the dock. The gray, flat-bottomed sky pressed the chill across the water.

"There were no caskets. Most funerals in this coast village did not require them. Men who died aboard ship were cast overboard in weighted canvas bags. In this official company gathering, nobody tried to explain how the men died, and no one explained whether they were formally committed to burial at sea or lost to the ocean. All there was to be shown for the years lived on the ship were a few items making individual bundles tied in faded shirts, for release to the widows.

"The ship's officers in lockstep, shoulders almost touching, eyes straight forward, approached the widows on the open dock, and handed over the dingy bags, and a share of the seasons earnings. There were a few whispered words to make sure the correct women were being addressed. There was no touching, no personal condolences, and there was no prayer or service.

"The black man they called Adam had no woman on the dock to claim his bag. Among his possessions were thirteen gold nuggets which had been pierced and strung together with reindeer sinew. Between each nugget was a flat, ivory disk. Each nugget was the size of a molar. A note found in his possessions read, '*In the event of my death I leave my life savings to my friend and shipmate Val, the carpenter. He is aware of the place where my savings are kept and the manner in which they can be accessed. He may do with them as he wishes. My gold bracelet, I leave to my shipmates for them to decide how best to share it among themselves.*' As the crew expected, the officers put disposition of the bracelet into the hands of the Chief Boatswain's Mate, the senior ranking non-officer on-board the ship.

"Finished with their official business, the officers turned away from the crowd and marched in lockstep, heels clicking on the paving stones, knifing between the mourners, cutting away from the pier. They quickened their pace, heels striking the uneven planks of the dock in unison, all stepping together, all making one hollow sound as they passed under the gulls that hung in the air and cast shadows on the dark water.

"The carriage that waited for them was shiny and clean and looked out of place. The carriage was hitched to a fine pair of chestnuts with full manes and combed tails. It had shiny brass lamps along each door and curtains to seal out the weather. It rode on straps and springs that kept passengers insulated from the jarring of the cobblestone streets. Inside, the seats were upholstered with imported fabric and there were soft, clean-smelling comforters to keep out the chill. The driver wore a red and black uniform with high black boots and a gold shoulder braid. His black top hat was jammed tight down on his forehead. He had one hand free for the horses and the other held a long whip. The carriage also had a footman dressed in the same attire, who helped each officer aboard then swung aboard the rear of the carriage and planted his booted feet on a black ledge filigree.

"Everyone knew the officers would hurry directly to the company office. That is where the owners waited, and they had sent the carriage. The carriage was provided to retrieve the officers as soon as possible, and the officers knew that they would have to find some other means of transportation back.

Without a word, the driver clicked his tongue, snapped the reins and they drove off quickly. A black sky began to pour rain.

"The ship's 'carpenter,' as you should have guessed by now, Hecky, is an important part of this story, and you will recognize his name. This handsome, strong, young man, Vladimir Baronoffsky, was your great grandpa, and he had made a survey of the *Beluga* prior to its departure on this ill fated voyage. He had documented each and every discrepancy he found. Some of the discrepancies were serious, so Baronoffsky had the survey made into a formal report with instructions to his solicitor to provide a copy to the owners.

"Fearing they would have to pay a large sum to bring the *Beluga* up to standards, the owners had promptly destroyed the document. The survey was intended to be used in part to support the carpenter's request for specific materials needed to repair worn or failed rigging and running gear, including the failed block and davit which had later caused the four deaths at sea. When the list of materials was shown to them before the voyage, the owners dismissed the survey and the request for repairs as frivolous and too costly. The repairs were ordered to not be done, and the officers forgot about it.

"Baronoffsky's solicitor had kept a copy of the document, and now it would prove to be of significant value. Upon the vessel's return, Baronoffsky instructed the solicitor to visit the owners and 'sell' them the copy of the survey. The owners did not have to be convinced. They could see a sympathetic court, or worse, an antagonized local population that could cost them a great deal more than the price of the paper. Fuming, they opened their purses to buy silence and safety.

"Baronoffsky took the proceeds then dispensed them to the families of the lost seamen. Despite his desire to keep a secret, somehow word of what Baronoffsky had done spread among the crew, and Adam's bracelet with its thirteen gold pieces was tied around his wrist in the night as he slept.

"In a drunken jovial mood months later, the solicitor told

the story to liven up the local inn, and of course he swore everyone in the place to silence, which only guaranteed the story's fame. By morning even the neighboring villages had heard of this ship's 'carpenter,' the man called Baronoffsky. Within two days the owners heard the story from the local newspaper owner who was trying to get the owners' side of the story before printing it on the front page. The owners cringed at the thought – a ship's carpenter had dunned them for four dead men. Even worse, they looked like fools. They tried to blame the deaths on the carpenter, because the *Beluga*, with him aboard, had just sailed again, but the solicitor soon cleared up the matter and the newspaper got the story straight.

"The owners vowed to get even. If Baronoffsky did not return with the *Beluga* the villagers would miss him, but the owners would likely never admit he was ever aboard the vessel. If he did return, he would be without a berth on any of the company vessels in the future, and very likely without pay for the voyage.

"But now I need to return to the castaways, who were by now cold, and hungry huddling on the windswept knoll above the ice filled bay. You can see now, Baronoffsky knew the ships officers would have no incentive to return for him. He guessed they already knew what he had done, but still he looked far out to the horizon. There was nothing but the wind.

CHAPTER 7

The Encounter

Wind and sea, an eternal pair,
Forever heard beyond the pain,
Surround me with the ocean air,
I am comforted by the ocean rain.

It was time for Baronoffsky to search the beach again for debris from the sunken longboat. Earlier, he had retrieved his shoes and a blanket that he spread over the bushes to dry. For him, the climb down to the beach was not difficult. The notch in the bank, which was nearly invisible from the beach, was not as steep as it appeared from below. There were many places his longer arms and legs could reach to hold onto. The notch made a steep but natural sand and stone climbing route. Footing was slippery and a fall would be possible if one was not careful, or if one was too small to reach the handholds.

"Halfway down, Baronoffsky saw a body lying on a kelp-covered outcropping that jutted out from the side of the notch at the bottom. Someone had fallen from the slippery stones that bordered the nearly-hidden notch. Alive but not moving, the person breathed shallowly. He gathered this person and a small bag of belongings into his arms, his heavy breath filling her face as he struggled up the notch. Near the top, as he set foot on the grassy outcropping which had been undermined by eons of wind and water, the sand gave way and his smooth-soled shoes that worked so well upon a pitching deck would not grip the slope. He held tight to the limp figure in his arms. As his feet slid out, he fell forward but protected her against the weight of his body. Climbing the stays aboard a ship, it was second nature to grab and hold on for safety's sake, and his reaction now was to thrust his hands into the soft earth as he fell against the undercut bank. Baronoffsky's feet dangled in the air as he fought to gather strength to pull himself to safety. His breath came more heavily, his heart pounded and fluttered, and his vision began to dim. The figure in his arms stirred, and the movement threatened to push them both over the edge. Near exhaustion, he worked one hand free of the earth, grabbed her fur garment and pushed her ahead using his shoulders and arms. As he thrust her over the top of the bank, she became suddenly alert.

"Breathless and weak from the climb, he was unable to say anything. She turned, and her black eyes looked upon his sand speckled face wet with sweat. She looked at the trail their bodies had made on the cliff face and saw how the trail ended in a vertical drop one hundred feet above the beach. She extended her small hands and pulled his shoulders. He heaved himself to the plateau beside her and rolled over heavily next to her. He looked at her and she slid her hood to her shoulders. He could feel the softness of her female body and was surprised by it. He raised himself to his knees and studied this person who he knew could scarcely weigh one hundred pounds. Her black hair was long enough to disappear into the fur parka. Silky, clean and straight, it moved softly in the wind.

"She had never before seen a man like this. She did not know if he was a demon or a god, and her throat tightened so much that she could make no sound. Her gaze found the pale eyes looking into hers and they were telling her, 'Be calm, I am good.' They were bright and deep, set in a face that seemed to have no color. His brows and gritty hair were the color of dead grass, and his skin had a pinkness about it without which she would have thought he looked the color of the corpses she left behind days before.

"She moved closer to him and said in a near whisper, 'Queanna,' and he nodded. He, too, had reason to thank her, and said 'Thank you.' She recoiled at the deepness of his voice. She was aware of her throbbing temple – it was swollen and blood crusted from her fall. It would be alright if she did not move too quickly, she thought.

"Baronoffsky had been a man of few words aboard the *Beluga.* There was not a great deal to talk about with a crew that seemed to neither know nor care about the world beyond the ship. The sea was their life and they made up simple explanations for the things they did not understand. Baronoffsky stayed out of conversations that explained events by the phase of the moon, the birth of a child, a thing done wrong, or some other superstition of that sort. He had little hope of impressing these men with scientific explanations, for they had grown up with superstitious beliefs and valued them as knowledge. Those who did not accept folklore could not be trusted, so Baronoffsky kept to himself his knowledge of geography, biology, medicine, astronomy, and the great works he had come to know as a student at the Universities in Kiev and Paris years before.

"As he looked at this small face, words rushed from him. He could see there was intelligence in the black windows of her eyes. He gathered himself up and reached to help her to her feet, but she was upright and stepping back even before he could draw his hand back from her elbow. She felt safe in turning her back on him, and she did so as she reached for the bag now on her shoulder. She retrieved a dried piece of caribou meat and offered it to him. The morsel was salty and spicy and he ate ravenously. He was not sure what it was but she gave him words as he ate, and she described in her language how it was made, and where it came from. He began to feel his energy coming back to him, and he began to recount to her who he was and from whence he came. Intelligent people can easily make themselves understood with hand signs, but the two of them added words, wanting to learn each other's language.

"Minutes later they were at the shelter entrance and the fire had burned very low. Baronoffsky fed some dry grass while she pulled away the matted grass from atop a nearby hummock. She reached into the earth and gathered an armful of nearly dry peat and put in on the fire in small pieces, giving words to what she was doing. The fire began to smoke, and after a few moments, flamed hot and steady. She piled grass and willows on the backside of the open fire and directed the heat into the shelter. She saw movement along the rear floor of the hut and became alert to the other survivor.

"The other survivor was weak and unable to sit or stand. He had not been gotten out of the water fast enough when the boat capsized and had a bad cut on his scalp, besides having almost suffocated while being dragged under. Wilson was his name, but he was so far gone he could not answer to it.

"The girl backed out of the hut. Her head throbbed, as she searched around the tall grass outside the hut. She did this until she found a frail, woody bush with shiny dark brown leaves that had not fallen off with the coming of winter. She gathered two handfuls of the leaves and stems and dropped them into a skin pouch she took from her bag. She filled the pouch with water from the stream near the hut, and from the stream bed, gathered stones that she placed in the hottest part of the fire. When the stones were so hot they might burst, she rolled them out of the fire, and pinching them between wads of grass, dropped them into the pouch. In moments, the pouch was steaming a medicinal brew. She produced a cup made from what appeared to be a whale vertebra. She took a sip of the brew and passed it on to Wilson, whose head Baronoffsky held up. Moments later he was alert and wanting more. He ate some of the dried caribou meat and pulled himself nearer to the fire, but a siege of coughing robbed him of this momentary victory and left his nose and mouth oozing foamy blood. He had many broken ribs and Baronoffsky had wrapped them well, but even so, there was little that could be done for the ragged ends of bone poking through his pasty, swollen skin.

"When Baronoffsky looked at Wilson's injury, he remembered an event in an earlier voyage when a storm had hurled itself against the *Beluga* for three days, creating seas so enormous that a man could scarcely bear to look up at the high, black, thundering mountains. The screaming, howling, wind shrieked through the rigging – loudest in the middle of the roll – changing to a growl when she was down, and kept up day and night. Ice collected on the ship, coating everything, making her top heavy and as she rolled in the sea, the motion became slow and dreadful, as if she would not come back.

"It became too much for the ship to take, and the constant pitching, smashing waves, and weight of ice combined to loosen the weather-side mast stays, snapping the top mizzen. A broken top stay had fouled the gaff, and began to tear the rig down. Heavy blocks, a mast timber, and a gaff were swinging with each roll and loose lines were snapping like bullwhips. Then a weather side stay came loose and fell over the side, trailed alongside, then fouled the rudder. Unable to stay hove to, unable to steer, the ship plunged straight downwind into the troughs running faster than the waves, threatening to broach deep and roll to her death.

"The deck crew scampered to rig a sea anchor to slow the out-of-control ship as the tons of twisted broken timbers, jumbled blocks, tangled chain and rope swung overhead. Each roll of the ship whipped the gaff, sheets, and torn sail against the stays, promising to plunge the remaining mast and booms to the deck and probably through the hull below. It would take pure luck for anyone to survive the icy trip aloft, and even more luck to free the broken rig and lower the tangled mass to the deck without being killed by the thrashing gear. The crew hoped the broken rig would free itself and crash into the sea, but they knew such things never happened. Even with death of the ship nearly certain, out of fear, all the seamen turned away as the order to go aloft was given. The captain held his hand on a pistol tucked into his waistband and ordered the mate to unlock the armory.

"Looking upward, Baronoffsky pushed himself through the group of downcast faces, but as he began to climb the rigging he was thrust aside. The shove caught him off balance and he tumbled to the deck where he lay gasping for air, the wind knocked out of him. As he rolled over and looked up he could see Adam had stepped out of his galley and pushed him aside and was climbing aloft before the officers could declare anyone guilty of disobeying a direct order. By the time the mate returned from the armory with two loaded weapons to enforce the order, Adam had reached the first broken yard and was able to snag the whipping sheet and make a hitch to anchor it around the mast. The deck crew speedily tied it off to the gunwale so that the mast was steadied. He did this again with the loose top lift and the running stays fighting to hang onto the wildly swinging, pitching jumble of timbers and canvas. With the mast steadied, he kept climbing and made fast the higher halyards and sheets, using them to anchor the broken rig.

"In a few minutes he had stabilized the most dangerous breakage, and others began to climb aloft. Climbing down with stiff fingers and numb feet, he was slow to move out of the way of a still swinging block, and took a solid hit across his ribs beneath his raised arm. Hurt, he fell the last fifteen feet to the deck and was unconscious, ice in his wooly hair shining like a crown of glass beads, open lips showing white teeth, arms and legs open to the heavens. His jacket had ripped open in the fall, and two gleaming white ends of bone showed that his ribs had given way. Baronoffsky quickly sliced the skin and set the bones in place, then bound him so he would not hurt himself more. He awoke as Baronoffsky was placing him in a bunk.

"Adam was strong, and there was no infection. He was

back in the galley five days later, and for the next three weeks two of the crew were in the galley whenever he was there. They fashioned a padded keg for him so he could rest and heal as the volunteers did the galley duty.

"Wilson had always been one of the weaker ones. Wilson's chest was caved in and his injuries were obviously far more serious than Adam's. Bones poked through the skin, but the real damage was his punctured lungs. Baronoffsky felt there was nothing he could do. Wilson looked very gray and his skin was wet and clammy.

"The girl did not expect him to live more than another day. In her mind she could see the faces of the dead villagers. She made a pad of grass and soaked it in the remaining tea, than pressed it on his open cut so that she could painlessly close a flap of torn skin on the crown of his head. She tied the wound closed by knotting his hair together close to the scalp. She wet the pad with the rest of the tea and pressed gently against his open chest wounds. Wilson began to relax and breathe more easily.

"Baronoffsky was taken by the ease with which she acted, and impressed that her actions had definite and immediate positive effects. She talked throughout, and he explained to her in English his understanding of what she was doing.

"Her language was thick with sounds of p, q and k, but they were made deep in the throat and hard to duplicate. It also seemed the same word, or series of words, had different meanings depending on how loud or soft certain parts of a word or phrase were uttered. He found there were many different ways to say the words for water, or snow, but still it was the same word. One needed to be very careful, since the way the word was pronounced, how loudly or softly it was said, how much it was drawn out, told where the water was, what kind it was, hot or cold, fast or slow, salt or fresh, rain or river. One word could be used to tell if snow was light or heavy, old or new, blowing or falling, dry or sticky. He would never be quite sure he had the correct emphasis on any of these, and was embarrassed more than once when she broke out in a grin and giggle that rolled into a hearty laugh. He judged he was not doing well on his pronunciation of body parts.

"His way of speaking seemed like a monotone to her. How could words be clear unless they were properly said? He spoke to her in his language quickly, and did not laugh. With each attempt he taught her something different, and she remembered. She learned more quickly than he. In an hour, they each began to pick out and use words of the others language.

"They knew Wilson was fatally ill and they had done all they could for him. They made a warm place for him next to the fire, and during the night he stirred delirious in the darkness, screaming names Baronoffsky thought must be demons in his dreams. When the dawn came, Wilson coughed fitfully again, then stopped breathing. They placed him in a depression at the bottom of a slope, and covered his grave with stones. They kept his heavy winter clothing for themselves and left the body in its light shirt and seaman's pants. Wilson's belt still held the sheathed knife every sailor kept handy, and Baronoffsky removed both it and the belt. Wilson was a Christian, so Baronoffsky said a prayer, and his companion said nothing.

"Hecky, this young girl's real name was Sukaruk. This name meant the 'strongest one' and she was to become your great grandma, my mother. Baronoffsky had no doubt of her strength, but he wondered why they did not name her the 'pretty one.' He would call her Sukaruk even years later, in places far away, when others would know her only as Susan. She was from a family of hunters, and hers was one of four families in the village. The village had been on the coast of the Chukchi Sea since ancient times, and the graves of the ancient ones had been the power to which the villagers prayed. For centuries, they had no contact with the outside. No one in the village had seen white men, though other native families that passed through told stories of different-looking people with the strange language, clothing, and foods. In the village where she was born, she had lived sixteen years. The world she knew was small and personal, both loving and harsh, and to her always beautiful.

"Now I wonder if you realize how close you are to the life your great grandma led and the people she knew as her entire world before the day she met Baronoffsky. These things happened less than one hundred years ago, and if she had not stumbled across Baronoffsky in the wilderness, perhaps you would have a different name and be living in a village along the Arctic seacoast, or more likely neither you or I would have ever been born. You might be feeling better at the moment, though, for it is so cold up there, and the winters are so long, that there are no trees. If you lived there you would need to depend on the sea to stay alive, and even as I tell you this in the middle of the twentieth century, there are many people who are close relatives of ours still living much like their forbearers did. Your great grandma was always happy with Baronoffsky, but she always wanted to return to her home, and eventually she did. But that part of the story is yet to come.

"As a child, she traveled only as far as nearby berry camps in the summer and fish camps on nearby rivers in the spring and fall. The entire village went together as if one family, and to a great extent it was. An intelligent and curious child, Sukaruk sought out the village leaders with questions. Their answers entertained her as a small child, but when she was about eight years old she began to realize their answers did not explain the world as she suspected it really was. She knew if she shared her thoughts with the elders they would not understand, or worse, they might think she had lost faith in them and become treated as if she lived outside the circle of the tribe. She did not want to be cast out of her only family, so she did not take issue with the elder's teachings. She hoped someday the mysterious white people she had heard stories about would come to the village, and that they might be able to answer her questions in a different way.

"That same morning after burying Wilson, she and Baronoffsky stood on the grassy hill top and looked out to sea. The wind was gentle now the air had warmed, and there was no sign of rain. Visibility was good and they could see twenty miles out to sea. The ice field had been scattered, but even with the danger gone, there was no sign of the *Beluga*.

"Hecky, you need to go lay down now. You look like you are not very comfortable and the doctor said you should be resting in bed today, anyway."

My arm throbbed and the swelling on my face had gotten so bad I could not see anything except the floor in front of me. I hated to leave the story because I knew she was just getting started, but I could not bear the pain much longer; it was like a tide itself. I wondered what Grandma expected me to do. I felt a little inadequate, especially since I needed help to get off the chair, up the stairs, and into my bed. I told her, "Grandma I really feel like I want to know more about them. Will you tell me the whole story about how we are as strong as the tide?"

"Yes, and tomorrow I will tell you the part about the trek."

"Huh?"

"You need to know how we got from the Arctic to this great city. You will see that was no simple thing, and the story will let you get to know them each much better than if I just tell you about them. I think this is because each of us is made up of things we do. So when you have an opportunity to experience something new, do it well."

CHAPTER 8

The Trek

I was awake early the next morning because I wanted to hear about the trek, but I would have been awake anyway. I hurt more than I did the day before, and I had slept very little. My arm and shoulder would not let me get comfortable. I thought a broken arm was a big deal yesterday, but I was now of the opinion that the a dislocated shoulder hurt so much it might be fatal. I could not dress myself and had a hard time even going to the toilet. I hurt so much that night I thought about peeing in the bed.

Grandma knew what to expect. When I got to the door of my room, she was there to help me. She had a quilt and pillows fluffed in a rocker she had pulled in from the parlor, and right away she fed me hot chocolate, aspirin, and toast with soft boiled eggs. I didn't think I liked soft boiled eggs, but they were so good I asked for more as she started the story again with a poem. She began,

"A chain of marks, made in the sand,
Not now alone in the frozen land,
But paired and tied by a turn of fate,
They shall, not now, the tides await."

She paused and looked at me for a moment and fluffed the pillow. I felt more comfortable than I had all night and except for anticipation of the story, I would have closed my eyes and taken a nap. I had thought about the trek much of the night, and needed to hear it.

Grandma got up and fed the stove a shovel of coal and turned down the damper. I felt that she was about to have me lie down again so I tried to look wide awake. Then she sort of smiled as she settled back in a chair facing me. Grandma knew me better than anyone else did. She ran her hand over my hair and began.

"They returned to the hut, gathered everything they would take with them and rolled it all into the caribou hides. They tied the bundles tightly, leaving straps at each end for shoulder slings. As a signal for the *Beluga*, should the vessel ever return, Baronoffsky built a cairn at the bluff where it could be seen from the sea, and inside, he placed Wilson's shoes upside down to signify death, and one after the other, signifying the direction Baronoffsky and Sukaruk would travel. He found a piece of driftwood to use as a mast for the cairn. The marker would be visible even after a snowfall. The sun had risen to midday before they got underway. The weather was good and they expected the afternoon to lead into a clear and moonlit night.

"It was difficult to walk in the tundra because the constant cycles of freezing and thawing had pushed the ground into willowy hummocks separated by watery ditches, and beneath the water was sticky mud. The travelers slid into the water every few yards, and the climb back onto the hummocks was far more difficult for Sukaruk. When she stood in the water, the hummocks were level with her shoulders, and she tired quickly, struggling to climb out of the mire every few yards. They changed direction and found the going easier in the well-drained soil near the edge of the bluff. Then they climbed down to the sea and made better time on the beach gravel.

"On the ridge above the beach, the wind made the grass dance in place. The breeze whispered its own quiet song, as if working to call forth the Arctic spring. Spring colors in the tundra are subtle and kind. When winter comes there is only whiteness and wind. Sometimes there is the dull crunch of moving sea ice, or a sharp report of pressure changes in the pack ice. The never-ending whiteness contrasts with the darkness, which lasts many days. The sun sinks below the horizon and abandons the Arctic to its winter. In the spring, new life creeps forth and bursts into color. New creatures flit about in the lengthening days, basking in the sun and fattening themselves in preparation for the winter. The flood of life which invades the Arctic in the early spring persists through the short summer until after the frost, when the colors become stern as the grasses and flowers lose their tenderness, and begin to harden themselves for the coming months ahead. Berries not gathered during the warm, long days shrink and dry on the stem. It is as if they know they must save themselves and will share their bounty no more.

"Now, as they traveled along the beach in comfortable strides, spring was upon them and the birds were beginning to return from far away lands. The richest season of the tundra was just beginning. The smooth sea washed over pebbles that glittered like jewels in the sun. The water made thousands of circles and dimples, each of a different color. The beach fetched ashore long shallow waves with each swell of the sea that rolled the pebbles about, and with each wave the mix of colors changed. In the late afternoon the travelers stopped for a moment to listen to the rattle of moving pebbles and to look at the sky changing colors on the horizon. Baronoffsky tried to tell her of the lands he knew beyond the sea but her known world was a few people, a village, the tundra, and the sea. He felt she might have to wait until she could see the lands for herself. She was struck by his knowledge and patience and felt that someday she would know this man perhaps better than he knew himself.

"In the early evening, when the tide was at its slack, they harvested clams to steam. They picked them from among the kelp, and in a deep pool rimmed by rocks, they gathered a large red crab.

"Near dark, they noticed pieces of wood scattered along the high tide line. This was not driftwood worn smooth by years of sliding against pebbles and sand, but hewn timbers with sharp ends and split edges. There were many fragments. A mile farther, they came upon the bowsprit of the *Beluga*. The ship had not been able to clear the ice pack and had been caught, then carried into the rocky shoals by the force of the ice against the hull. Some of the offshore reefs warned of their presence, showing spires above the water like churches, but the crags hiding just under the surface were hidden headstones that ripped out the bottoms. Helpless against the storm and tons of ice, the ship broke apart, probably first losing its top rig then holing the hull in the battering against the rocks and clenching crush of the ice field. The force was too much for even the greatest ship to withstand and even the best of all crews would not have been able to break free. The launching of lifeboats became impossible with the rig down and the ship over on its side to leeward. Baronoffsky knew this because the wreckage was badly splintered and scattered a long distance across the beach. If the *Beluga* had run aground on the beach or sunk free of the ice field, the wreckage would be more concentrated and there would be some hope of scavenging supplies or even a longboat. He and Sukaruk camped near the wreckage and watched as the sea washed over the remains.

"Baronoffsky told the story of the ship. He could not tell if she understood that this had been his home and, in a way, his family. She had never seen a ship, but she repeated many of the words and stopped him twice with questions. That night he built a large fire from the wreckage and allowed himself to recall his lost companions.

"Sukaruk sat up with him late into the night and wondered if there was a way to count the stars. The sky was so black the stars seemed to go on forever. She thought to herself these same heavens have been looked at by her parents and their parents and everyone who walked the earth before them. The elders called the stars spirits of the dead. She wondered what they would make of the blackness between.

"Before she slept, she pulled from the fire some of the long, thin, curved pieces of the ship and tested their strength against her knee. The ones which broke she threw back into the fire. The two that passed the test she put aside for the morning. She moved near Baronoffsky and listened to his breathing. She placed her head upon his extended arm. His breathing did not change as he folded her close to him and turned his body to share his warmth. She no longer felt alone.

"In his slumber he became aware of the softness and warmth next to him, and he began to dream. As a wisp of her hair brushed his cheek, his dream took him to memories of Paris. He saw richly dressed women along its quaint and majestic boulevards. There were fancy women in stately carriages, dowagers with their young charges, loud women in the fish market, and ladies of the night. In his dream it was springtime and the blossoms were out. Swans glided across ponds as couples shared company beneath the billowing trees. A woman's laughter floated across the grass and the sun warmed his back as he stretched his arms around her waist.

"Then in the dream he was at the opera with his friend, Maurice, with whom he had roomed while a student at the University of Paris. They did not go to the opera or theater often, but Maurice felt it was important to be seen and known by the Paris aristocracy if his career as a supplier of fine silk and lace was to follow the path he had divined for it. Maurice was a thin but handsome young man with a gift of having people like him at first meeting. Such a gift could be used well in his chosen career. He was not the kind of person to go anywhere alone for he loved to be in the company of others. Baronoffsky on the other hand was standoffish and guarded in his relations with others, and had been reserved in his contacts with the opposite sex. They often shared their fantasies about the women they saw in the Paris streets, because even in this magical city it was difficult for outsiders to meet women of status. This night, Baronoffsky was to be Maurice's guest and they had a box at the opera from which they could see the entire stage and also look across the way to the opposite boxes. There was a lovely woman in a lacy white gown by herself in one of the boxes. A gas light burned above and behind her. The light cast shadows about her hair, and he could see it was nearly black. During the opera, the lady in white received what appeared to be a note that she looked at quickly, then tucked away. A short time later flowers were delivered and she set them on the floor, nodding, but saying nothing to the deliverer. She sat alone through the opera and was joined by a very small but sturdy looking lady of the same age as the end came near.

"Her gown was cut modestly in front but her breasts were obviously round and full. Her waist was so small it seemed that she should break in two. Her face was that of a goddess – green eyes, full lips around a pouting mouth that revealed even teeth that gleamed when she smiled. Although alone, she smiled often at the performance.

"As the curtain came down, Baronoffsky excused himself. He rushed down the gilded stairs and across the lobby to wait at the kiosk in front of the theater, for he knew the lady in white would have to pass him there. Sure enough, she passed, smoothly making her way through the crowd, looking straight ahead. She seemed to be smiling as a footman helped her into a grand carriage in which the other woman was already seated. As the carriage rolled away, he followed on foot. He kept the coach in sight, sometimes having to run, through the winding, gas-lit Paris streets. He soon found himself breathless. As he rounded a corner into a narrow alley, gasping and choking for air, he saw the carriage come to a stop in front of a house with a steep roof and what appeared to be a large, private garden in back. The carriage attendant helped both ladies from the carriage to the house and bowed as they disappeared behind the arched timber door. Baronoffsky stepped closer to the house as the carriage pulled away into the night, and he could see flickering lights behind the draped windows, and he heard laughter.

"The next day he sent a note to the address of the lady in white, introducing himself and begging to have her company. In his fantasy he imagined her running to him, but the common sense part of him did not know what to expect. He was startled from his studies by a knock at the door. It was the lady's masculine-looking female companion. She had in her hand the note he had written. Her companion, Marie De Paris, she explained, was a kept woman and she could see him only at great personal risk. Regardless of who he was, and she certainly did not know, she would be putting at risk the fine manner in which 'the Count' kept her and this was a risk she would not give away for free. She went on and on about the cost of living in the style that Marie required and to which she had become accustomed. She said Marie was living for the time she could afford to escape to America, and wanted to start a new life in California.

"The Count seemed to be a generous though obnoxious and demanding man, more of a fat clown than a lover. His wife was even older than he, and the source of his wealth. She had warts on her body, spreading for years until they covered her hands and face. She rarely went forth during the day and kept to herself on their country estate. They had no children. The Count was a lonely man with access to more than enough money to hire good company. The ladies feared that he could be a jealous man, and since both Marie and her companion lived well off of his generosity, she had come to warn him off.

"So it seemed to Baronoffsky that he was in love, deceived, then discarded, all in the space of a day. He was affected deeply by the experience and would attend the opera often thereafter just to see her from a distance. She acted as if she did not know who he was and treated the flowers he sent as she treated the others, leaving them on the floor at the front of the box. He was aware that her companion recognized him, as she looked at him often and turned to speak to Marie seemingly without expression. He led himself to believe Marie knew of his feelings and enjoyed them.

"Then one evening she was not at the opera. From his place near the corner of her street, where he had taken to watching the house, he had seen her leave alone in the carriage an hour before. When he returned to his room having walked off his disappointment, she was inside waiting. Her scent filled the room. She caressed her cheek against the ball attached to the bedpost. Her nearly black hair held quiet strands of red within it. The gas light made her shadow dance across the walls and ceiling. The flame made changing shadows on her face, then she reached over and put out the lamp. She began to remove the buttons of her gown. It was that night about which he dreamed.

"Next, Baronoffsky felt the hard sand beneath him and smelled the campfire burning. Sukaruk was already up and moving around on the beach in the dawn of a clear calm morning. Before he awoke, she had fashioned two hunting bows from the pieces she saved from the wreckage of the *Beluga.* She had cut long, thin strips of the caribou hide for the string. She also cut a few willows and skinned off their bark, then hardened them in the fire. Many birds were nesting so feathers were easy to find. In the morning, she showed him how straight and far the arrows could be shot. She was surprised – the bows made from the *Beluga* were light, but stiffer and much more powerful than those she had made in the past. As she showed him these things he watched and listened, then he gave them names in his language and she repeated them back.

"The bay in which the shore party had been sent off from the *Beluga* was itself within part of the arm of a long peninsula that jutted west, far out into the ocean. Baronoffsky saw no need to stick to the beach any longer. He was more interested in heading to the south even if it meant an overland trip. He explained that there were places far to the south where they could find others of his kind and hers as well. There were many people in some of these places, but they were a great distance away. Still, they could be reached before the snow came again. In his mind, he had visions of swollen rivers to ford and wondered how they would cross when the time came.

"They would be traveling in the long days of summer. Game would be easy to find, but they made themselves busy gathering an emergency food supply, anyway.

"They journeyed past a small stream where salmon entered at high tide, so they built a weir of willows and stones. The fish would find the opening in the weir, then become trapped by the willow fence. Baronoffsky scooped them out as they crowded together at the upstream end. By late afternoon they had captured two hundred fish, each weighing in excess of twenty pounds. They cut fillets from each and returned the carcasses to the ocean. They scooped a large shallow depression in the sand where they built a roaring fire which they fed until sunset. Then they knocked the coals into the hole and covered them with a light layer of sand and two layers of seaweed. The fillets had been soaking in the salt water until now, and they were placed on the seaweed with a sprinkling of leaves she had gathered from low plants near the campsite. These were covered with more of the flat seaweed and buried with sand. The fish was left to steam and smoke the entire night. The next day she and Baronoffsky removed the fillets from the pit and mounted them on willow grids left to dry in the fire smoke. By the end of the second day, eight hundred pounds of fillets had been reduced to about thirty pounds of flavored, dried fish that would keep indefinitely. Smoke-flavored and leathery, it was delicious and full of nutrients.

"The dawn of the following day, they bid goodbye to the seacoast and headed south across the tundra. Their path took them over a landscape of rolling hills, where the melted snow and ice did not create either hummocks or a quagmire. Each hill, however, had rivulets of snow melt to cross. Their feet stayed wet, but the small streams provided a dependable water supply.

"By afternoon they could see in the distance a plume of white steam, and as they continued in its direction, a pungent odor penetrated the air around them. They saw a green and blue barren slope rolling down from a low hill. The slope looked like mud, but as they drew near they could see it was stone and it steamed with tiny, shallow pools of foul smelling water. The pools became wider, deeper, and hotter higher on the slope, and they climbed upwards until one of the pools continually filled itself with water that flowed upward from a crack in the bottom. The pool spilled hot water over its rock rim into many smaller pools below. Baronoffsky put his hand into the water. It had been many months since he had a hot bath, and his body, now accustomed to the cold and wet, might not be able to take the steaming heat.

"He removed his coat, then his heavy shirt, and plunged his arm nearly to his shoulder. He held it there to test the heat and found it to be much warmer than the air but only hot enough to provide rest and comfort. He turned to place the shirt on top of his pack. Sukaruk was kneeling there with her garments folded at her feet, bending and reaching toward the water but enjoying the steam around her legs and body. Her hair was longer than he had imagined – it tumbled in loose fluffy waves to her waist. She was small but extremely strongly built. Her muscles rippled when she moved, and even her flat stomach had a band of muscles. When she bent over, the skin across her abdomen stayed smooth and tight. Her legs were straight and shapely, with strong calves and smooth knees. Her thighs were round and powerful looking. When she rose for a moment to her feet, she stood in a way that kept her shoulders back and square. He found himself staring and tried to look away. She seemed pleased he had noticed her and smiled at him, showing her even teeth, and her eyes sparkled. He was stunned by the smooth velvet look of her skin as she slipped into the deep pool.

"She was a year beyond the age at which the people of her village became mothers. She had been slower to develop than the other children, and the hard winter slowed adulthood as well. She noticed herself becoming a woman in deep winter and the changes took place more rapidly than she expected.

She was comfortable with herself and felt strong and young.

"Baronoffsky turned toward her from where he knelt beside the pool, and she saw the purple scar running from his heart across his chest down the center of his body to his belly. She gasped. There were small tracks running across it as if to hold him together. She stared as he shed his garments and rolled beside her into the pool. She lightly touched it and asked, 'How was this body so broken?'

"He was taken aback at the clarity of her pronunciation, but even more so by the completeness of her grammar. Then he realized she had only learned from him. He had been careful to avoid the pidgin English traps that irritated him. He was aware of her bright spirit and intelligence, but even so, he was surprised she had been able to form a question. He had talked with her incessantly in his language explaining things, naming things, and talking, always talking as they walked. There had been two weeks of a nonstop, twenty-four-hours-a-day language immersion, and it showed in the quality of her question.

"He had not noticed or thought about the scar for many years. His mind reeled back to the dream of the night before. The opera, Marie, Paris, and the Count rushed through his mind. He felt a need to tell the whole story, and as he went on, they moved from the pool to the warm, smooth rocks to lie in the sun. When the wind dried and chilled them they returned to the water. She was captivated by his description of the city, its grand scenes, the boulevards, the shops, the theater, the parks, the University, and things called books and letters, in which one's thoughts could be reduced to marks on paper for others to read. She learned many new words and allowed her imagination to create pictures in her mind as he talked. They both wondered, for different reasons what had become of Marie, and was she alive. She seemed to have a hold over him, for his speech slowed and his face flushed every time he spoke of her.

"The dream he had the night before always ended the same way, for what happened next was too painful to recall. The dream would become vivid almost real, and never changed. On that Paris evening as Baronoffsky and Marie embraced, the shadows danced upon the walls and peals of laughter rolled into the small room from the bistro across the plaza. Marie folded her body around his in a passion that caused his heart to beat strong. She removed his clothing, kissing his shoulders, and held her head tight against his torso. She pushed his body back against the high feather bed and dropped her gown to the floor as she crept over him. Her breasts brushed his cheek, and her skin was silky in the faded light.

"The Count was indeed a jealous man and not one to be made a fool of, nor was his wife. The Countess of Warts, as he would forever after think of her, feared that if he did not have the comfort of Marie, he would most certainly leave Paris, and this she could not bear. So it was the Countess who hired street ruffians to rid Paris of the young Baronoffsky. Following her instructions, they broke into the room and stabbed and slashed Baronoffsky, putting him at death's door. The innkeeper and his wife heard the screams, breaking glass, and thrown furniture, and rushed to save their inn. The ruffians pushed them to the floor and dragged the naked Marie downstairs into the street and threw her into a waiting carriage. Upstairs, the innkeeper saw the blood, and thinking Baronoffsky was dead, poked at the still body. He rolled face-up, causing the innkeeper to recoil at the sight and run into the hall.

"The inn was a gathering place for other medical students like Baronoffsky, and one of them was summoned to close the wound. There was a great loss of blood, and intestines bulged from the wound. Deep, coarse stitches were needed to close him, then other layers of stitches to close the skin itself. He was still alive the next day, and by the day after, was unconscious but still free of fever and infection. In time, the wound healed and the crimson scar was easily hidden under his shirt, but there was no covering up or chasing away the pain of the broken heart that had remained with him all these years.

"In a fit of depression, Baronoffsky quit his studies. He

signed on aboard a sailing vessel at Le Harve, bound for Boston. By chance, the vessel was built and owned by Americans and sailed under the name, *Sarafin.* All of the crew except him had been with the vessel since New Amsterdam and were homeward bound. Most of the crew were immigrants themselves not long ago, so they made the vessel a happy place for newcomers. The captain was glad to take him on for free passage as a doctor, or at least someone who was nearly a doctor. He was expected to be of great value for a trip like this, which was sure to have many passengers. Countless immigrants were seeking new lives in America, and the *Sarafin* was going to be loaded with them.

"When the story about the scar was finished, and the answer about the scar was clear, Baronoffsky was very tired. As he gazed upon Sukaruk's smooth skin and shimmering hair, he felt old.

"Sukaruk looked closely at this man. She was beginning to understand him. She thought she knew more about him than anyone she had known before. No one before had taken the time to answer her questions, but he gave information without her asking. She marveled at how much he knew. She wanted to hear everything, and she wanted him to be happy.

"By Baronoffsky's own choice he had spent years upon the sea, some of it in the southern ocean with days under the hot sun. The crew spent many hours shirtless in the open sea, and the elements tanned their skin to a leathery satin. His body had hair all over, soft and smooth but standing away from the skin in tight curls. The effects of the weather showed mostly on his face, even though protected by an ever-present beard trimmed close. Still, his face with its scars made him appear to be older than he was. In Sukaruk's village, a man of thirty-two would have been an elder, and certainly would be boasting of grandchildren.

"They rested in this place for two days. During that time she asked many questions and his answers were long and complete. Her curiosity was about him, and she fashioned her questions in a way that had him telling of his likes, his dreams, and where he had been and things he had done. She remembered everything.

"Before they fell asleep she asked him, 'Baronoffsky, will you walk with me to this place you call Boston?'

"The question caught him by surprise and he tried to stifle a laugh as he pictured them walking across Alaska, Canada, the Washington and Oregon Territories, and the United States. He couldn't stop the laugh, and she was embarrassed. He realized he had not really talked of geography, and she knew nothing about it. By the time he finished explaining the geography of the planet and where Boston was, his throat was dry and raspy. Still, though he went on, for he needed to explain why he would never return there.

"Boston was the place the *Sarafin* made landfall in America, and would be the place new immigrants could begin to make homes in a free land. The voyage went uncommonly well. The weather was fair and the ship comfortable. He was given a dry and well lighted cabin next to those of the captain and mate. The three spent many hours together. Baronoffsky's cabin was small but infinitely more comfortable and private than other quarters on board the *Sarafin* which by standards of the day was a good vessel; with a fine and compassionate crew. By the time the voyage was over and the *Sarafin* had tied up alongside the wharf in Boston Harbor, Baronoffsky had delivered four babies and lost no patients. He was in good spirits as he stepped onto the wharf among a throng of merchants, craftsmen, and fishermen chanting and waving to get attention to sell their wares. He reveled in the energy and satisfaction these people showed – they were enjoying the freedom of doing what they wanted to do when and where they wanted to do it. He felt good from spending time with good people committed to making a future for themselves and their descendants in a new world. The new immigrants flooded from the ship, and as they took in the busy scene, many had tears of happiness rolling on their cheeks. Baronoffsky was proud to be a part of their journey.

"As he walked through the throng and neared the street at the end of the pier, he noticed between the planks a black man chained hand and foot. He was standing ankle deep in mud and his back was scarred and scabbed. The barnacle growth on the piling showed that when the tide came in, if the man were left there, the water would cover his head by more than a foot. Worms from the piling had crawled up his arms and were beginning to eat at the dying flesh of his back.

"The black man held his head high and stood quiet and still in the shadow. On the pier above him, a kneeling man with bulbous nose was trying to lower a sign around the black man's neck. The sign said, 'Uppity Darkey For Sale.' The man's red coat was too small for him and the open front revealed a dirty but once fancy silk shirt.

"As he heaved himself to his feet, the man looked down his wet, red nose at Baronoffsky.

"Baronoffsky asked, 'Is this man a murderer or thief?'

"The fat man laughed, and from his too-tight pants pulled a flask that smelled of alcohol and drank from it. He released a foul smelling sigh, coughed, then spit a brown liquid on the dock. It splattered against Baronoffsky's boots and dripped through the planks onto the black man below.

"''Worse', he said. 'This one, he tries to act like a white man. He likes to be talkin' quiet and clear like he knows what he's asaying, and the worst part is, he looks you right in the eye wilst he's adoin it. He don't show no respect at all.'

"'But what did he do?'

"'Do? DO! What he does is act uppity, and we won't have them acting better n' they is. I cain't even sell him, why I'd be selling him fer ten dollars if'n he don't up n' die on me first.' The man held one nostril with his index finger and blew a shot of mucus out of the open nostril, catching his lapel. He brushed at it.

"'Hugo Low don't need no ten dollars, but he shore don't need no smartass, dumb black, either. I'd just let the worms eat him there but they'd be too slow.'

"Baronoffsky pulled ten dollars from his pocket before the fat man could start talking again, and waved it in front of Hugo. The fat man wheezed and drank from the flask again, and chuckled to himself, 'Hugo, you old fox, you alright, you done it agin, yes, yes, yes.'

"As Hugo was congratulating himself, Baronoffsky bought the key to the lock and also the black man's chains for one more dollar. Fat Hugo Low nodded his agreement as his body jiggled with the enjoyment of selling a human life. Baronoffsky listened as he walked Hugo to the deep end of the pier as he went on loudly about how the 'darkey' kept telling everyone he was from Portugal, was not a slave and never had been one. As the two men stood at the end of the pier, Baronoffsky held the eleven dollars out over the edge. As Hugo reached, Baronoffsky moved his long arm out just a fraction of an inch more. Leaning forward with both arms waving, Hugo toppled into the water with the eleven dollars he batted out of Baronoffsky's loose grip.

"Hugo surfaced choking and gasping, nearly paralyzed by the shock of the cold water. 'I'll get you fer this. No matter where you is. I'm gonna find you. I'll burn yer house down, I'll git yer whole stinkin' family. Fire is what yer gittin'.

"Out of earshot, under the dock, Baronoffsky unchained the black man, who when asked said his name was Adam, and brought him to the *Sarafin*. The Sarafin was empty of its crew now and would be moored at the pier for the week in preparation of the next voyage. As they boarded the polished deck, Adam tottered with fatigue, and Baronoffsky thought of the cruelty he had left behind in his own Czarist Russia. Adam's family were probably aristocrats in his native land, but in this new place he had experienced bigotry because of the color of his skin more than any other single factor, or circumstance.

"He could discuss important events, in at least two languages, and he was aware of the great works of literature. His knowledge of business and trade was amazing and he could read and write. When the captain returned five days later, Baronoffsky introduced him to Adam. Adam talked plain and simple to the captain and the captain was impressed with the way Adam looked him in the eye. 'An honest man,' he thought. The captain was surprised he could sign on a crewman with these credentials and did so because of the need for educated company on board during the long trips. Adam shipped aboard the *Sarafin* as the cook, and he and Baronoffsky did not see each other again until many years later, in California.

"Baronoffsky explained to Sukaruk that he would not willingly return to a place where townspeople allowed such cruelty. Some other day he would tell her about the gold and ivory bracelet tied around his wrist. He had seen her looking at it before but he knew there were more important things in her mind. She rose up on her knees and silently began to knead his back. He began to fall asleep, and was not sure if he was awake or dreaming when he heard a soft and gentle voice say, 'Perhaps I will be your Marie.'"

I slept much better that night because I knew Grandma was going to tell the whole story. I could see she enjoyed the telling at least so long as she had me there to pay attention. The doctor came by and left something to help me sleep, and it was very late in the morning of the next day before I was fully awake.

When I finally got to the kitchen, Grandma was ready for me. My breakfast was a huge stack of pancakes and a hot chocolate. She had fashioned an armrest of a pillow and cardboard box that kept my arm and shoulder comfortable as I sat in one of the high-backed chairs at the kitchen table. I did not have to ask her to continue the story. She asked me if I wanted to hear more. I was hooked and she knew it, but still I couldn't help myself.

""Yes, yes, we can't leave them all alone in the Arctic. I know they must have lived or we wouldn't be here." She tried to hide her enthusiasm, but she gave it all away when she started talking more quickly than I'd ever heard her do before.

CHAPTER 9

New Friends Among the Old

She started, "The most valuable thing in your life will be the people in it. Some will not be your friends, but never stop trying to treat everyone as if they were." She recited a poem.

"True friends are made strong and fast,
They come in colors, and sizes that vary,
True friends are among the things that last,
False friends are those who are never merry."

Without pausing, she continued the story.

"The nights were becoming shorter as the Arctic summer approached. Soon there would be no darkness at all, and then they would be able to see the sun work around the horizon in the middle of the night. They would push themselves to walk longer each day to take advantage of the good weather and longer hours of sunlight.

"The wildflowers began to spread their carpet of many colors. Some of them had come out so early that they bloomed through patches of snow and ice. One day there was a field of ice in the distance, and as they walked toward the horizon for hours in the sunlight, it changed color before their eyes. The flowers overpowered the forces of winter, blooming even as the sun melted the ice away. Their fragile leaves, stems, and petals seemed as if they could not stand against even the summer wind, but their seeds survived under the snow and ice year after year. In the clean, Arctic air, their colors were vivid and blended as if in the style of French Impressionists. They danced and waved to silent music, seeming to say, 'See me now, touch me now.' Their life would be short and soon their colors would disappear with the frost, stems stiff and brown. But for now, all nature hailed their beauty. Their legs pushed through this carpet of color as they walked steadily southward. There were colors and plants to name for each other. Sukaruk told him about their fruits and roots and about their uses. He was amazed at the medical storehouse beneath their feet. They made brief stops to gather plants and roots; one root was taken for sore muscles and joints, another for the pain of headache, another for fever, one for infections, one for ingrown nails, one for bites, one for energy, one for constipation, one for severe pain, one for skin rashes, and so on. Only tiny amounts were needed, and when all were gathered, they were barely enough to fill his fist. She assured him they were adequate for a year. He hoped they would only need to depend on these things for a few weeks at the most.

"Birds became more plentiful by the day. Ducks and geese arrived in flights of thousands. They could be heard long before appearing in the sky even on the clearest days, and they landed nearby, unafraid of travelers. They took two at a time with the bow and arrow, and eventually found they could walk up to them and stun them with a stone. The birds had no fear and much curiosity. The two travelers continued their journey hour after hour, day after day, talking while their bodies became used to the pace. They had little need for rest, and even enjoyed exploring the ridges and streams.

"Near nightfall, four weeks into their journey, they felt as if they were being watched. Tiring, they were careful to make camp near the top a hill from which they could see well all around, even though this meant they would have to pack water from the stream in the valley below. They built a small campfire for an evening meal of roast duck and tea. Then as the moon rose, they heard wolves for the first time.

"Sukaruk recoiled at their howls, which seemed to be getting closer. She remembered the attacks in the village the winter before. Here they had no place to hide, nor dogs to protect them. Baronoffsky felt a hint of the danger, for he had heard stories of packs of rabid wolves that ventured into the winter streets of some European villages.

"As the sleepless night wore on, the howls and growls came closer. Bristling bodies appeared in the dusk, silvery fur reflecting the firelight. One by one, the wolves began to show themselves. One the size of a man stopped and gazed at the pair, than sat back and howled as if to make his presence clear. The pack became excited and the howling intensified and quickened as others joined in. The wolves could be heard in the brush, moving in a closing circle. They worked continually to build the fire higher, and tossed smoldering clumps of peat out to the perimeter.

"There were twelve agitated wolves working closer and closer. The large one with its yellow eyes and snapping jaws seemed fearless it was less than thirty feet away. The rest of the pack began to take places behind the leader, like an army of the mad. Baronoffsky stared at the leader's huge open jaws as the grey body bristled and stretched toward them forcing he and Sukaruk to back closer to the fire. As it crept forward and snarled, Baronoffsky released an arrow into its gullet from fifteen feet away. The arrow found its way into the wolf's open mouth and buried itself in its pink throat. The mouth closed, feathers barely showing outside its muzzle. Baronoffsky notched another arrow and hit another of the pack. The arrow struck behind the ribs as it sulked past. It poked through the animal's torso, and the animal dragged itself into the dark on its front legs. Two more wolves came out of the shadows. He and Sukaruk released arrows at the same time, and both wolves fell. The howls had turned to yelps of wounded animals, and the rest of the pack, perhaps another eight or ten animals faded into the twilight.

“There was no sleep to be had that night as they sat back to back near the fire, alert, with arrows notched and bows ready. As the sun came fully above the horizon and brought the full light of day with it, they counted four dead wolves within yards of the fire. Baronoffsky kicked at the leader’s carcass, and Sukaruk could be strong no more. She collapsed, her body heaving with dry convulsions of fear and exhaustion. He recognized immediately what was happening, for he had seen this in others, and in himself after the incident in Paris. He put his arms around her. He stroked her head and back, and talked to her in his deep, soft voice. He made a comfortable place for her by the fire. He let her rest and cradled her in his arms as the sun took a lazy arc into the sky. The midnight sun highlighted the cirrus clouds, which formed like strands of cotton, then painted the strands in silver.

“He began to understand how important this creature was to him, but he wondered if his feelings would be the same if he were in Kiev, Paris, or Boston where his acquaintances and lady friends were fashionable, educated, and older. But he was here now and so was she. Still, he had never known anyone like her before. There was more to her than any woman he had ever known. She awoke and looked at him as if to say, I am so sorry, but before she could make a sound he kissed her there amidst the waving flowers, the Arctic sun, and a thousand geese flying low across the horizon. She held to him tightly and snuggled against his chest. She said to him, ‘I shall be your Marie.’ He thought to himself, ‘One day you will be my wife,’ and he did not know why he felt a lump in his throat and tears in his eyes. They caressed one another and rested until the dawn of the following day.

“Every night thereafter they gathered extra wood for a large fire, for they felt this to be their best defense against the wolves that were probably after their food. They would also make and have ready more arrows. They would never again be taken by surprise, and he would do nothing to put her at risk. He began to wonder if there was such a thing as survival of the fittest. The strongest of the wolf pack, the leaders, were the first to venture into danger, and the first to be killed. Perhaps the influence of man had upset the natural process of the wilderness. If he were back at the university, this would be the very thing which would interest him, but he put it out of his mind and vowed to be careful in assessing the risks he and Sukaruk would take lest they, like the wolves, became bolder than life allows.

"All traces of snow and ice were gone from the ground except for the deeply shaded places at the bottoms of ravines and on the steeper hillsides. Willows sprouted forth and the entire landscape took on a softer look as the breeze rolled ahead of the travelers making the willows and wildflowers bend in waves. Willows seemed to grow thicker and taller with each day of travel, and the days passed without event. They spent hours side by side, with Baronoffsky talking and teaching, and she listening, repeating, and learning. There were many times when their path was marshy and tangled. In these places they walked single file with Baronoffsky always in the lead. He was much taller and his height provided a good view of the terrain ahead. There were always choices to be made about which way to go and it was best to make these choices before the going got so difficult that they had to backtrack. He was always alert for bears, though they had seen no sign of large animals except for the migrating caribou herds. If they were to stumble upon a bear the encounter would most certainly be in the thickets of berries and roots. They skirted the areas they could not see into and beyond.

"As they crested a low hill early on a cold, overcast, morning, the landscape faded before them. The rolling hills coasted into a shallow, broad valley and in its bottom was a stream braided by many channels. The water was brown and gray tumbling over enormous rocks that forced the dirty water high in the air then plunged into whirlpools and eddies. The spring weather and rain of the past two days had caused the stream to rise out of its banks, and now the weather was cooling again, the rain had stopped and the flow would diminish. It seemed unlikely the water would ever become clean. He wondered if in the winter the water became gray and brown ice.

"Sukaruk had never been to this place before. The river was greater than any she had imagined, but she knew enough about the land to explain that even the rivers flowing from glaciers are always cloudy and rarely muddy. The nature of a glacier is to have a river below which is milky green. The river they were looking at was brown, so she said this was not from a glacier but caused by flooding from the recent rain. The rain together with the rapidly melting snow caused the waters to roil, and soon the waters would become quiet.

"Even as they talked, the river began to quiet itself. In two hours the flood no longer swept through the willows above the bank. In four hours the river flowed within its banks, and in the places where torrents had roared in foaming cascades, the water now flowed fast but quiet. They made camp near a spring on the hillside and watched with great surprise and joy as against the horizon a faint pillar of campfire smoke appeared in the fading light. As the evening fell, the river began to change again. The water rose with the nearby ocean and reflected the celestial power which drove the tides.

"The soft light of the late night sun was still visible low on the horizon, accompanied by the ghost of a full moon. Between the cycle of flood and ebb, the river's many channels began to show the travelers a way across. They decided to cross each ribbon at its best point, moving up or down until they were at the other side of the river. They sat through the night as they watched the tides write their plan, and marveled at the pillar of smoke which they estimated was about two days distant. Baronoffsky carefully marked its direction using the stars and the sun so they could pick their course once they crossed the river. Then they heaped damp grass and bundles of willows on the fire and built great billows of smoke. In an hour's time, a heavier plume answered from the far horizon.

"In the morning, the ebb tide and quiet river allowed them

an uneventful crossing throughout which the travelers kept their food and belongings dry. They had made note of the shallows from their hillside camp, and crossed at those places when the tide had ebbed. They found themselves moving much faster and without tiring as the anticipation of an encounter ran through their thoughts and fed energy into their bodies. They did not stop to gather or prepare food the entire day, eating instead from the supply of dried fish and drinking from streams. The expectation of a two day journey shrunk to one, and the plume of smoke guided them closer. Then beyond the next rise they could hear voices and the barking of dogs. Then there were people pointing and children dancing about amid shrieks of excitement. The villagers crowded about and touched and poked them as they laughed. One lady held two happy children and all three giggled as another woman poked and felt Sukaruk's belly, but when she looked away and said nothing they became quiet.

"Sukaruk began to explain where they had come from in her language. The people of her village used the name Kakarak among the elders for many generations, and this village traced its roots from the same family. She was united with a newfound family, and they treated her like royalty. As she recounted her story there were many different cries of 'Unikahaw!' and 'Ezihagee!' each with a slightly different accent, and some exclamations drawn out short and others long. So Baronoffsky could tell Sukaruk was making him out to be bigger than life and enjoying the embarrassment of it.

"Baronoffsky was a head taller than anyone in the village. The sun and weather had darkened his skin, but his wild blond hair and blue eyes made him an oddity among the people, most of whom had never seen a white man. Those who had traveled to trade skins for white men's things were less happy to see him, especially with one of their women. There was an undercurrent that made Baronoffsky feel like an outsider more than he had at any other time in his life. But they were friendly and gracious and had a great deal of respect for the odyssey Sukaruk had described.

"The village held a period of mourning for Sukaruk's family, and as the sun dipped in the sky, the men began to beat their drums slowly and chant a funeral verse. They said the same words over and over, 'I-I-I-Un-gah, I-Un-gah, I-I-Ungah,' with variations of rhythm, accent and duration. The women and some men rose up and began a slow dance, facing each other in a circle. They waved their arms and moved heads so slightly left and right that the signs could barely be noticed. They stomped their feet in cadence with the drum beat. They did this from a low crouch. Baronoffsky noticed that the delicate hand signs and rocking movement of the dancer's bodies contained the telling of a story and a salute to each dead person.

"When the dancers were done, they drew Sukaruk into their midst and encircled her with their arms. The circle quickly opened with her in the middle. The drums began again and she began to chant and tell the story of loss of the *Beluga*. At its end Baronoffsky was led into the middle, and around his neck the oldest grandmother placed a necklace of caribou sinew on which was strung the fangs of a wolf and the claws of a bear. He was given the name 'Ee-tee-yait,' Great White Bear.

"The village was a summer fishing camp where the villagers caught and dried salmon for the coming winter. They would stay in this place until late summer, and then move the camp to a place where they could gather berries, and then move again to a place where they could hunt in the fall. Finally, before winter arrived, they would move to the seacoast where they could hunt seals and fish through the ice when the cold winter months made fishing in the rivers and gathering berries impossible. The furs they gathered would be used for clothing, and any extra would be taken to the trade post by boat – a three day travel to the south on the open ocean. Such a trade trip had been planned for a few days later, and Baronoffsky and Sukaruk were urged to come along before they even asked.

"In preparation, the trade party planned a two day trip to the coastal winter village site. From there they would depart by boat for the trade post. When they arrived at the coastal village, Baronoffsky and Sukaruk were put to work with four men from the village and two old women, examining the skin boats and making them ready for use. Baronoffsky was pleased with what he saw and impressed with the care and workmanship the villagers put into their boats. These people would leave little to chance while on the open ocean.

"The winter camp was on the beach where the villagers constructed the boats. They were made by fastening together delicate driftwood frames with carved interlocking joints tied together with strips of walrus hide. The boat frames were covered with walrus hide then shrunk tight to add strength. The boats were light, pointed at each end, and paddled by everyone. They had a fine bow and high freeboard. Their sparse frame and skin covering made them light-footed in the sea, so people had to remain seated and move about as little as possible as the boats settled and surged with the power of each stroke. The trip to the trade post always took place in late summer, and when they arrived at the destination the villagers would wait as long as necessary for the supply ship to come, for the supply ship delivered the goods they desired most. The village needed a rifle.

"The dawn came, and the *Umiak* – as they called it – was pushed off the pebble beach. Everyone settled into the easy regular stroke that moved the boat forward with a swish of water against the translucent skin hull. From time to time, someone shipped his or her paddles to attend to other duties, but the boat's progress was steady and dry. The boat would be paddled nonstop to the trade post with a round-the-clock effort. The villagers sought no harbors or stops unless an emergency forced them ashore. Always there was the sound of paddling and the villagers resting in their bench seats in shifts of one, two, or three at a time. Unlike other boats Baronoffsky had known, this one did not leak water into the bilge. The villagers stored items directly on the bottom as if leaks were unheard of. Food and drink were available when needed, and whenever someone stopped paddling to catch a short nap, the boat's speed did not vary. Baronoffsky's practiced eye saw that the course was consistent even with the turning of the tides and shifting of the winds. He felt comfortable with this strange craft and crew as land fell from sight behind them.

"The crew leader was named Ooginak, which meant 'Wolf Pup.' Command of the boat belonged to him, because he had harpooned a whale from it the year before, and that was the only whale taken that season. A successful hunter became 'owner' of anything that helped him make the kill. Even the crew of the boat became 'his' crew. The boat-builder was his brother, Newlookin. The brothers did not yet know at the trade post they would vie for the attention of the trader as if there were only one rifle in the world, even though they had furs enough to buy five rifles, and everything else the village wanted. They did not know they would try to show their bravery by drinking from the trader's whiskey, and they did not know they would squander the furs in drunken foolishness.

"At the end of summer the *Umiak* would have to return to the winter camp. During the trip the brothers would drink the white man's whiskey and fight over the single rifle they had given a year's worth of furs for. In a drunken contest of marksmanship they would shoot up all of the extra cartridges. That winter the rifle was useless due to lack of ammunition, and would be used by the old women to chop holes in the ice, and the empty cartridges would be pounded into arrowheads to hunt more furs.

"The arrival of the *Umiak* at the trade post was not the only event of its kind. Many native skin boats arrived from other far-flung villages throughout the summer, and the native camp town that had sprouted up on the beach grew each day. The trade post itself was inhabited only by white people, and Baronoffsky was an oddity to both sides, since it was unusual for a white man to live among the natives, and unheard of for a native to live among the whites.

"As the villagers in Wolf Pup's *Umiak* began to set up camp at the edge of the beach settlement, three white men from the trade post walked down to look the group over. They had seen the crew of the *Umiak* approach, and Baronoffsky had caught their attention. The three approached slowly, three abreast, and halted two paces away from the native crew, which was unloading the *Umiak* and pulling it ashore. Looking only at the tall white man the center, one said in Russian-accented English, 'We would like you to come up to the store and join us. I am sure we have much to talk about. Who are you?'

"'I am Vladimir Baronoffsky of the brigantine, *Beluga*. She was lost in the ice far north of here weeks ago, and I am the only survivor. This young lady is Sukaruk and I owe her my life. These other people are from a village less than three days away across the open water.'

"'Yes, we know them. They have been here before with their dirt and noise. Someday they will stay at the far end of the beach on the cape so the wind from their camp does not blow their stink this way. The lazy savages want to stay here all summer. Some of us have our families here, you know, and we don't want their influence on our children.'

"Sukaruk moved forward from the center of the villagers and as she stepped closer to the trio, she interrupted in unaccented English, 'Sir, I am from a village far away, and I have no need to stay here long. I hope you are happy here, for this can be a place of great beauty. My people say happiness comes from within.'

"Out of the side of his mouth the man in the center muttered, 'Now here is an insolent bitch.'

"Another said, 'The slut can learn how to empty a slop bucket, they all smell like it anyway.'

"Then, 'Wonder who the hell the klootch thinks she is, God or somebody?'

"They were speaking in low tones, their heads turned so the

wash of the tide against the pebbles, the slight wind off of the ocean, and the voices of natives on the beach stole the words out of the air before they could reach Baronoffsky's ears. Because of this blessing, they would live another day. The three men turned to walk back to the trade post, waving over their shoulders for Baronoffsky to follow them.

"Baronoffsky learned in his meeting with the white occupants of the trade post that they were lonely people, but even so, desired to keep apart from the natives. One man, a Russian Orthodox priest named Ivanoff, committed himself to 'civilizing the savages' by converting them to his brand of Christianity, and so he did everything possible to impress them with his sincerity, which on the surface appeared to be genuine.

"Father Ivanoff was from Kiev, the city of four hundred churches. Baronoffsky knew the thousand year-old city well. He and the priest had many things in common – among them, knowledge of the arts, and appreciation of chess. Ivanoff had sewn together a cloth chessboard, and had carved a set of chessmen in great detail during the long, dark winter months. The set was an incredible work of art in green soapstone and gleaming ivory, but the men of the trade post were not interested in challenges beyond checkers and cribbage, so the set languished in its cloth jacket.

"Ivanoff was the only single man there, and the only man of the cloth. Religion was not important to the rest of the whites, but because Ivanoff's mission depended on the natives giving up their beliefs and culture, he railed at them for their pagan ways and the white people were thankful for his presence. He was a boon to the trade post business because he spent his energy convincing the natives to accept a new way of living. This included not only religion, but customs, food, and dress as well. The traders, of course, supported the priest in talking the natives out of their furs and into calico. The calico sold well, at least until the first winter, and the natives discovered how quickly calico caused them to freeze to death. Nevertheless, they desired the colors and patterns, and after the first winter began to use pieces to decorate their garments. It was not unusual to see a native person dressed in furs under a loose-fitting calico cover up, or fur clothing with geometric calico decorations sewn into place as if they were part of the fur. Unlike animal skin garments, calico needed frequent laundering. So Ivanoff's attempt to civilize the dress of the natives not only compromised their protection from the cold, but the prized cloth made them appear to be more dirty and ragged than before.

"Ivanoff had little patience with any ideas but his own, and this was the quality that made him a valued priest. This was also the reason he was so far from home. As a child he was always an exceptional student, but unrelenting in his arguments with others. His stubbornness with his parents was a source of great unhappiness to them, though to some outsiders he appeared to have tenacity in his dedication to ideals. When he became a teenager, his parents were glad to see him off to the church for schooling, and did what they could to send him as far off as possible. He had been a lonely child – always taller, thinner, more sickly and more awkward than his classmates – and in this place he was still friendless. He tried very hard to befriend Baronoffsky, and they spent long hours discussing the sights and treats of Kiev. For a man of the cloth, Ivanoff did not miss out on the pleasures of the flesh. Indeed Ivanoff immersed himself in off-color stories told with a fervor that made them seem more imagined than real. Ivanoff, through his own confessions, tried to get Baronoffsky to confess a past that was not there, and Baronoffsky grew ever more uncomfortable with the conversations.

"Baronoffsky belonged to a Kiev family whose roots traced back over six hundred years, and at one time was very wealthy. His father was a high level government official with a distinguished military career behind him. He had lived a portion of his life in St. Petersburg, where he learned French, Spanish, and became a noted violinist. The family had a tradition of honesty and pursuit of excellence in all things.

"It was both his father's position in the Russian judiciary, and the younger Baronoffsky's powerful mind and body that admitted Baronoffsky into a regiment of the Imperial Guard studying governance at the age of eighteen. He soon rose to the rank of captain and made many friends among sons and daughters of important people. But he knew his talents were greater than the challenges he was being given. After a term of five years, he left to pursue medical school in Paris with a family blessing. He conducted his life consistent with the code of his family and the Guard, and he was by all accounts an honorable man.

"During Ivanoff's confessions he listened with patience but dissatisfaction. The man was on the edge of dementia and Baronoffsky shared nothing personal of himself.

"Ivanoff was careful to deprive himself of the luxuries that would appear obvious to others. His gauntness added to the impression of self sacrifice, which his carefully camouflaged vanity strove to attain. He often examined himself in privacy, a ritual he pursued with almost religious conviction. He used a handheld mirror, and admired his body by the light of a candle.

"Having few friends among the whites, Ivanoff relished teaching the young people of the village. That is, he held individual sessions with the girls, especially those early in their teenage years. The native custom was that couples were joined to each other when they had sexual intercourse, and that was as close to marriage as they got. This was of immense interest to Ivanoff, who would spend hours talking with the giggling girls in an attempt to extend to them the morality of the church.

"He soon was captivated with the free attitude of four young ladies and they became regular, private students that winter. Now that spring had arrived, he began to worry that his indiscretions would begin to show through their lighter summer wear. He confessed this to Baronoffsky.

"Ivanoff was an accomplished chess player, but his matches against Baronoffsky lasted as long as any of the matches he had played in Kiev. Baronoffsky began to win occasionally, than with increasing frequency. The more he won, the more Ivanoff insisted on playing. The game became an obsession to Ivanoff, while with Baronoffsky the pastime was merely a polite interlude that allowed conversation and relaxation.

"Ivanoff felt isolated from everything he valued. He failed in his attempt to civilize the natives for some froze to death in their calico garments. He had failed at representing the church, though nobody yet realized how badly. He felt unloved, and now he was failing at his most prized accomplishment, Chess Master.

"In the privacy of his quarters, he wrapped the chess set, and attached a note. 'As my only earthly belonging, I bequeath this to Master Baronoffsky.' He laid out his Bible, crucifix, and garments, and attached another note. 'To my beloved students I bequeath these Heavenly possessions.' No one saw where he went, but in the morning he was gone.

"By late summer, Ivanoff's four unmarried students would gave birth to healthy children. They would be light-skinned, and one would have blue eyes. Civilization brought a new kind of outcast to the trade post, the bastard half breeds. If the natives were aware of this, they did not react and showed the same love and respect to these new souls as they did to all of their family."

Grandma let out a long sigh saying, "Hecky, do you know how it is my skin is dark, and my hair is black?"

"Grandma, I know that my great grandma was a native, so you and I are too. But isn't that a good thing? Is that where the power of the tide and the ocean comes from?"

"Yes, that is a good thing. That will always be a good thing. The power of the tide and the ocean comes not from being a native, but from the strength and love your family has within itself, for the sea, the earth, and everyone on it. Inside of yourself is the strength and wisdom to look beyond a person's color, religion, and beliefs to find the good things you have in common. To do any less is to disrespect humanity."

I thought about that for the rest of the day. I felt like there were a few things I might need to patch up with some friends I had judged too quickly, and probably unfairly. In the heat of a baseball game a week ago I had hit a home run. I knew I was safe at home but the umpire called me out. I stomped off, muttering, “Fat old man,” to myself. The umpire didn’t hear me, but now I felt guilty. All he was trying to do was to help us kids have fun. We had that in common and it was like I hated him for it. After all what difference did it make if I was safe or out? None, really.

CHAPTER 10

The Discovery

Grandma began to prepare lunch, and as she talked, she steadily moved about the kitchen. She sang in the soft clear voice of a much younger person. She sang about the ocean and how it held the powers of life, how the sea held the colors of the rainbow, how the depths ringed all the great lands of the world, and how it gave strength to those who ventured upon it. Soon, a steaming bowl of clam chowder was in front of me with a piece of her fresh baked bread. She continued the story, starting again with a poem.

"Built with lines, strong and straight,
Built to sail, in the dead of night,
Built to stand, in the strongest storm.
She is fastened with love, and brass kept bright,
She shall sail with pride, and shall not wait,
Upon the tides, to be wind born."

She went on. "It was early morning in the beach camp when the travelers in the *Umiak* began to awaken and start another day. Though the sun hardly fell below the horizon that night, the early daybreak came with streaks of crimson and ruby red, and then yellow, and a fresh breeze brought the cry from the trade post, 'Ship ahoy, ship ahoy.' A mast was spotted at full sail perhaps ten miles offshore. The vessel appeared to be a schooner rigged sailing ship, sails bright and tall in the morning light. It was the *Discovery,* one of the grandest vessels under contract to the Russian American Company. Baronoffsky could see the black smoke of the bunker coal climbing from the engine's aft stack against the soiled spanker sail furled on the mizzen.

"The *Discovery* was a splendid American-built vessel, fashioned by East Coast shipwrights out of the finest materials. Baronoffsky had heard of plans for her when he was in Boston six years before with the *Sarafin*. The *Sarafin*'s mate was seeking a position aboard the vessel and had been hired by the owners to supervise its construction. The vessel was to be a substantial ship with excellent (if not lavish) accommodations. There were plans to fit it with a steam auxiliary engine built in England. The vessel was built to ply routes from Siberia to San Francisco and Hawaii, with numerous stops between, as commerce demanded. With a massive sail area and deep draft, she was expected to be sea kindly and still be trim enough to run before the trades with a full load. The steam auxiliary kept her safe from being driven onto a lee shore, even in an unfavorable wind. She was in every way a sailor's ship, stiff, fast, and strong.

"The *Discovery* was sleek and clean, even in the distance, as she vaned into the wind at the offshore anchorage and launched small boats over the side. Puffs of smoke billowed from her decks as she fired a cannon in salute and hoisted colors to celebrate her arrival. The captain's launch was first ashore, smartly rowed in by a uniformed crew. The entire village greeted the launch as it neatly settled against the soft beach gravel, smooth white sides gleaming and as even as if built of marble. The *Umiak* beside it looked frail and dirty, almost diseased. Baronoffsky noticed, however, as the crew stepped out of the beautifully finished launch with its bright wood and brass, that all of them had wet feet from water that leaked into the bilge during the short trip from the *Discovery* to shore.

"In celebration of the arrival of the *Discovery*, the trade post officials were dressed in their best clothing as they marched single file to the beach where they made one side of a triangle. From their side of the greeting party, there were military type salutes to the crew of the *Discovery*. The third side of the triangle was made up by a casual group of native onlookers curious about the formality. The trade post factor and the captain of the *Discovery* exchanged customary welcoming gifts. The factor seemed uncomfortable with this role and the gift was tendered with a stiff body and frozen smile which had the look of being saved in the trade post all winter. On their side, the natives waved, smiled widely and looked sincerely as if they were greeting old friends. The *Discovery's* happy crew moved among the crowd to make conversation with the trade post officials and natives. They appeared to be genuinely enjoying the meeting after so long at sea.

"Surrounded by the excited crowd, the captain of the *Discovery* turned away from the trade post officials to greet some of the natives on the beach. Then he spotted Baronoffsky, whose shock of unruly blond hair stood out from the crowd as an eagle would stand out in a crowd of penguins. He was also a head taller than anyone else around him. The captain saw through the unkempt exterior to the old friend he recognized.

"The Captain was Francois Goddard, the former mate aboard the *Sarafin*. He had a ready laugh that rolled into a howl then gently built to a melodious roar, which often started others giggling and cackling even when they did not know what Goddard was laughing at. Even when he was reading alone he often smiled to himself. His dark hair grew tall in loose waves and curls that bounced as he talked, making his neck appear to be barely supporting his head. He always appeared relaxed, and once aboard the *Sarafin* when Baronoffsky went to awaken him for his watch, Baronoffsky noticed that even in his sleep he smiled. His principles were as pleasant as his demeanor, and everyone who knew him loved him, and strangers wanted to meet him. His life was like a light to others, and when it shined on them they felt better for it.

"Baronoffsky and Goddard had become friends aboard the

Sarafin six years earlier. Goddard was a French Canadian from Saint Malo, a small town in Quebec, but he had spent many years in Paris and had relatives there and in the French border town of Metz. He was a former officer in the French army. His mother's family was from Kiev, so the two men had much in common.

"Francois Goddard had been selected as the captain of the *Discovery* after supervising its construction, and had been with the ship since its christening. The owners were thrilled at the vessel's quality which had been the talk of the town since the day the shipwrights laid its keel. There had been enough straight, old oak already at the shipyard, ordinarily fine to use. But Goddard felt that his keel's wood had to be seen first as a healthy tree before pinning the lives of his men on it. The timbers in the shipyard appeared to be true and adequate for the job, but he did not know what kind of soil they had grown in, what elevation they came from, how fast they had grown, if they had healthy brothers and sisters and if they were free of disease. He would have nothing but the best in workmanship and materials, and for that reason, had felled four trees for the keel alone. He was equally particular in all other aspects of the ship. The yard began to attract other ship builders, who visited regularly to see how their jobs were really supposed to be done. The *Discovery* was a celebration in quality.

"The day *Discovery* was finished and the owners saw the elaborate owner's stateroom, they unanimously decided on the spot to make Goddard the captain. In the polished mahogany frieze around the cabin top Goddard had a craftsman carve names of the owners and their wives. The cabin sole was flawless teak inlaid with holly. The rosewood wall panels were decorated with portraits of all of the owners, and on either side of each intricately framed portrait were silver candlesticks in the shape of a mermaid riding a dolphin. The crowning glory was that he had brought the vessel in under budget and on schedule. When the ship was done the workers that built it held a party in his honor. They hoisted him on their shoulders, and would have done so even if he had not surprised them with a brass plate engraved with all of their names and birthdays which he had secretly inlaid in the center of the door to the captain's quarters. 'Cap'n God' they called him in the privacy of their quarters, and woe be it to the man who thought of him as anything less.

"When Captain Goddard realized who this bedraggled blond face belonged to, he rushed forward to embrace Baronoffsky. This time his ever-present smile was accompanied by a tear and a roaring laugh all together. As they embraced and slapped each other on the back, the trade post officials were still making stiff welcoming speeches. They spoke too loud, almost yelling, in an attempt to capture the captain's attention. The other two sides of the triangle were more taken by the display of sincere friendship taking place to the side of the assembly.

"As the factor's speech dragged on, Captain Francois Goddard put a cigar in Baronoffsky's mouth and lit it, then led him by the hand to the launch and ordered him to be delivered to the captain's quarters aboard the *Discovery*. The two had much to talk about, and as the launch waited, they stood and talked on the beach. The frigid tide crashed in and rushed across the beach. The salt waves pushed about them and washed the sand and pebbles over and around their feet. They seemed unaware, and Baronoffsky spoke quietly to Goddard, faces almost touching. Baronoffsky put his arm around the Goddard's shoulders and whispered in his ear. Goddard pulled his head back, dark curls dancing in the salt air. He smiled, then laughed a glorious, musical laugh. The hoot and chortle roared across the water to the party on the shore. Not knowing why, others in the group began to smile and giggle.

"Goddard clapped Baronoffsky on the back and stuffed a second cigar into his mouth. Humming a version of 'Allueta,' he strode back to the trade post officials. The wind caught his curls for a moment like a halo. He turned to wave at Baronoffsky, and laughed aloud into the wind.

"Baronoffsky gathered a few possessions, gently reached out for Sukaruk's hand. And helped her into the launch.

"The night before, he had visited the trade post and talked at length with the factor. As a result of his visit, he had traded in Ivanoff's chess set. The new owners planned to trade it piece by piece to the natives for furs. The natives valued the figures for what they thought was a special power, for they had belonged to a priest. The factor felt he made a good bargain for the Russian American Company, hoping to get a hundred good pelts in the end, and all he had to give Baronoffsky for the chess set was the only pair of women's shoes and the only dress not already claimed by the factor's wife. The dress was far too small for her girth and for that reason had stayed on the shelf, tied up with string, since the post was established. The factor's wife had tried on various occasions to stuff herself into anything feminine, and some of the garments traded out of the post had split seams and stretched fabric from her attempts to force the garments around her. Some things had fit, at least until she would try to bend or sit. This dress, however, was so tiny that she could barely get one thigh into it, let alone her entire body. The dress was sewn from a soft pink, tightly woven cotton, and accented with a white lace collar and puffy sleeves. There was a tight waist with sheer frilly trim, and the skirt was pleated but full. The shoes were also far too small for the factor's wife. They were white like the lace, and had slender tiny heels.

"The *Discovery* was spacious and more elegant than any working ship Baronoffsky had seen. There was another series of surprises, too. The navigator, at least ten of the crew, and the mate, were all friends from his voyage aboard the *Sarafin*. Goddard had claimed the owner's stateroom for his quarters, since the owners wanted the ship only to make money and had no inclination to set foot on anything floating unless tied to a dock. Each of the officers also had his own cabin, so there was one extra being used for storage. It was quickly emptied for Baronoffsky, as he would be ship's doctor as far as Seattle.

"The cabin was a work of art, and comfortable. It had a curved ceiling in dark oak trimmed with a small diamond shaped inlay of rosewood. At the rear was a square port made of brass inset with leaded stained glass which let in the light and fresh air. The design in the glass was of a rose. Colors of red, rose and pale green reflected on the cabin ceiling as light from the sun hit the water and shimmered the reflection about the cabin. The port could be dogged closed and shuttered to keep out the splash of rain and sea or could be held open to allow the fresh air in. The teak cabin sole had a crimson and blue Persian carpet and there were finely crafted built in bureaus with curved fronts and locking drawers. On top of one there was a white and blue ceramic wash bowl with matching towels decorated with the name *Discovery*. On the other there was a collection of leather bound books. Two polished brass oil lamps mounted on gimbals provided light for reading. The door to the cabin had a heavy brass handle and opened to a walkway which led to the wheelhouse, then down to the galley, and forward to the mess area. The bed was not large but there were two mattresses and a colorfully quilted high and fluffy down comforter. At the rear of the cabin was a small wood fireplace with a flat top for heating water. This was as much luxury as Baronoffsky had seen in over a year, and more than Sukaruk had seen or even imagined in a lifetime.

"As they embraced in the quiet privacy of the cabin, there were footsteps, then a knock on the cabin door. The cabin allowed almost complete privacy. Baronoffsky opened the door, and found the captain's cabin attendant with a suit of clothes and polished black boots for him. The attendant whispered, 'The captain wishes you and the lady he continually refers to as Sue and Susan to accept these as proper attire for the ship's doctor. By the way, he says, they are also appropriate when the captain performs a wedding.'

"Baronoffsky smiled at the renaming, but accepted it without comment as he slid the door closed and began to heat water on the stove. They were alone among friends. As the cabin warmed and the light smell and crackle of burning wood filled the air, they bathed one another in the warm water. The gentle rocking of the ship and slaps of ropes and rigging complimented the quiet creaking of the timbers. The Arctic light brightened the stained-glass window and reflected dancing colors off the wood paneling.

"'Sukaruk, he said, 'it seems our friends like you so much they are giving you a new name much the same as your people renamed me. By any name, you are indeed a very special person. I have never before in my life been as happy with anyone as I am with you. I find myself looking after you and trying to take care of you, even though I know you are stronger and more able than most men. I find myself dreaming of being near you when we are apart. When we talk, it is as if we know each other's thoughts before they are said. When I look at you, I see a woman more beautiful than any I have ever known. I did not think this life would find me wanting to have a family. I have never before known someone I would want to do that with, but when I see you and think of you, I cannot see my life continuing any other way. I love you more than I thought was possible to love and I want to be with you forever. Will you be my wife, and the mother to my children?'

"'Baronoffsky, when you pushed me over the top of the sea cliff as your feet dangled in the air, I saw deep into your eyes. I knew then as we first met we would some day become one person. I have never been with another and I want to be with you forever.'

"As the *Discovery* rolled gently at anchor, they embraced.

"The crew and officers did not return until late in the night.

"In the light of the early morning, she looked like royalty in the soft pink dress. Her small waist looked even smaller in the gathered lace, and the new shoes enhanced her legs. She balanced on them carefully, the sunlight through the colored glass shining red in her hair, and she turned to see her reflection in the mirror over the wash basin. Astonished, she studied herself. She stepped back and began to realize she could be almost anything she wanted to be.

"To Baronoffsky, the blue officer's uniform was a generous touch. The pants were a bit short but tucked into the leather boots, they were perfect. Baronoffsky took his place among the ship's officers, and with his military demeanor, added dignity to an already disciplined and professional ship.

"It was no surprise that the ship was equipped with a workshop and forge, for there were more metal parts and machines aboard the *Discovery* than any other vessel he had been aboard. He was able to find a craftsman onboard who would use twelve of the thirteen gold nuggets from Adam's bracelet to make two gold wedding bands and two solid gold bracelets, one large and one small. The craftsman wished to make them for nothing, but Baronoffsky knew he had befriended Adam aboard the *Sarafin* when the black man had first been hired as a cook. Baronoffsky insisted the craftsman take one of the nuggets because it had belonged to Adam, and they had been friends.

"The wedding aboard the *Discovery* was the ship's first such event. The occasion was held on the top of the pilothouse with the guests assembled all around below them on the surrounding decks. The ship's officers made up the wedding party, and the captain in his finest regalia, complete with a tricorner hat and military medals, performed the ceremony with great flourishes of his hat and arms.

"Susan chose the oldest grandmother in the beach camp to act as her matron of honor. The old lady did not fully understand what a wedding was as she stood atop the wheelhouse with these strange people, but she knew this was important to Susan. The old lady felt comfortable in her fur garments over which she had pulled a bright blue flowered parka. The fur of her mukluks trembled in the breeze and the calico parka billowed about her, making her look as if the wind had deposited her there. She clasped both arms around a huge bouquet of wildflowers. She was a bouquet of color herself among the dark, straight uniforms. Her broad smile showed two missing teeth and a weathered face that almost hid her almost black, eyes. She was less than five feet tall but carried an energy that created an aura of being at the center of things.

"Captain Francois Goddard wanted this first wedding aboard the *Discovery* to be special, so he told no one that there would be a cannon salute. This was the first Christian wedding the natives had ever seen, and they did not know what to expect. Father Ivanoff had not explained the details in his passion to convert the natives, so they stood polite, quiet, and unmoving. None of them understood all of the language of the ceremony, so when the groom kissed the bride, they thought the formalities were over. The cannon blast brought shrieks of excitement from the deck, the matron's bouquet scattered into a rainbow of flowers, and one junior crewman who had posted himself on the rear yardarm above the wedding party was so surprised that he lost his footing and hung by his arms until he could scramble to safety. Someone set off the steam whistle and the natives nearly panicked, ready to jump overboard. They calmed as the whistle became silent and the cannon echo faded.

"The native women began their cries of celebration and happiness, and a drum beat was started near the bow among a circle of native men. There were twelve of them shoulder to shoulder sitting in a tight arc on the deck with their feet straight out in front of them. They each held the handle of a drum, which had the appearance of short fat paddles. They produced a sharp, snare drum, rim shot sound that pierced the Arctic air, penetrating, ringing and washing over the people gathered there, the staccato beat sounding impatient and excited. The native women weaved individually through the crowd, converged, then made a semi-circle in front of the men, waving their arms and swaying to the drumbeat. They started a concert of voices in an easy, repetitive chant that flowed into the ocean and sky. It was a rhythm and chorus background for a dance in pantomime of the lives of Vladimir and his new bride.

"They pantomimed the giving of priceless gifts. In their language of dance, they gave her the strength to overcome the winter and burst forth with all of the beauty of nature, and gave her the strength of the sun which gives life to all. The high-pitched drumbeat quickened. The dancers gave her the knowledge and love of the spirits of her villagers that appear in the gentle breeze that caresses the sea, and which would fill the sails of the ship. They gave her the will of the tide, which can never be stopped, and they gave her the patience of winter, and the purity of the Arctic air.

"Then as some of them stomped in time with the drums, two danced showing Val as the Great White Bear. They gave him the spirit of the sun, for light was in his hair. They gave him the strength and power of the ocean, knowing the ocean delivered him from death, the ocean delivered him to his new wife, and it would be the ocean taking them to new places far away. Their movements gave him the skill and grace of the eagle, seeing it was in his eyes. They gifted him with the faithfulness of the tide, for it never fails, and they gave him the spirits in the wind to guide him safely through life.

"Susan took her place among the dancers, and the women closed around her and then the men closed around the women as all but one drum stopped beating. The group opened with Susan in the center, and the other drummers started again. She chanted with the drum as she danced, extending appreciation to the *Discovery*, the captain, officers, and crew, and then she danced and chanted her appreciation to the natives there. Her graceful movements and song conveyed her gift to them – peace, the winter snows that cover everything in silence. She danced to them the power of love, for it brings everything that is born anew in the spring. Her dance and chant gave them the protection that comes from the breath of the wind. In a crescendo of drums, her dance celebrated powers of the sea and mother earth to guide their hunts and keep them safe.

"She turned her attention to the laughing captain and they linked hands and embraced. As she moved and swayed almost imperceptibly, her skirt almost touching the captain, and her wind blown hair traced it's rhythm over the coat buttons of the officers who stood next to Goddard, she gently pulled them forward into the throng of celebrating natives. Their deep blue tunics and brass buttons mixed with the sun baked brown faces, calico, and fur. The natives handed the officers drums as they shot glances between themselves, nervous and uncertain what to do. One of the native men hit a leading drumbeat motioning at the officers and some joined in, reserved at first, then feeling the energy of the drum report, harder and harder. The native man started his chant looking at the officers and urging them to repeat. At first the officers held back, feeling awkward and embarrassed. Not knowing the language or meaning of the words, they kept their voices low. The native man's penetrating shrill voice driven by the staccato drumbeat awakened an inner primordial urge as the officers gripped the drums harder and held them higher. Their voices grew louder and harmonized as the native women joined the chant with them.

"Captain Goddard imagined himself dancing with royalty in a palace ballroom. He looked to the sky – the fluttering flags became the crests of many celebrant knights. The dancing natives became his soldiers and the drums became his marching corps. The emotion of the moment flushed his face red and made his eyes wide and glassy. He asked himself, *Where is my Susan, is there another like her, where shall I find her? Shall my life end with an empty heart? Such a woman as this can happen only once. She is the daughter of the wind and the sun. She is a child of the sea and the earth. She is from a people who survive the harshest climate on earth yet she is the most delicate yet strong and beautiful creature I will ever know. How can it be this way if she is from a place where the people are called savages by the traders, where they eat raw fish and meat. They live in fur garments and worship animal gods. These are the things which are within her and they are the reason she is what she is.* He caught himself frozen by the music, staring into her eyes, and spun himself back to reality as the drums became real and the signal flags called him back to the deck of the *Discovery.*

"Still on the top deck above the celebrating crowd were the white men from the trade post and their wives, who stood scowling and whispering among themselves. Such a disgusting display they never had imagined, or else they would not have come. It was beyond them to think natives could associate with whites, and had taken all of their patience to be present at the wedding. They rationalized that a boycott by the traders might have affected business and they misunderstood the motives of the captain and officers, thinking they were merely putting up with the outrage. Deeply disturbed by the idea of intermarriage and strongly opposed to it, they could think of no way to stop it. They decided they had to attend no matter how distasteful. They believed that such weddings would be a ruin of good society, were unchristian, should be illegal and that all natives were stinking savages unequipped to enjoy the happiness of civilization. They refused to join in with the celebrating crowd on the foredeck, keeping their commitment to bigotry untarnished, and crept away early. They were not missed.

"The entire crew joined in the celebration. A concertina, harmonica, and jew's-harp were produced. Soon a native drum joined with the other instruments and was beating a rhythm to an Irish jig as sailors danced about the deck with the native women, who were laughing and squealing happily. Then, in the late evening, as light begin to soften and spirits began to mellow, the music slowed and the men of the *Discovery* began to recall their weddings.

"'I remember the first time I saw my Meg.' It was the voice of McTavish. 'She was there on the Irish beach below the bog where I stood watching from the high road. She was leaning into the wind coming off the sea as the gulls hung in the air above her. I watched her open her arms to the sea, and the wind blew her red hair from her smooth skin. She didn't see me there and I would watch her often. I would walk by her family farm or see her in the church, trying to stand near just to smell her. I was in love from the first moment I saw her and we were married in the small church in the town above the water. All of our friends and families were there and there was hardly enough space to squeeze everyone in. What a wonderful party that was, music and dancing throughout the night. I love that woman every moment. It doesn't matter we are oceans apart for I feel like she is with me here and now. I can feel her and smell her in the night. She is with me on the ocean storms and in the cold of night. But still, I miss her dearly each moment we are apart.' His voice broke as he looked away from his companions, then out toward the horizon.

"'She does not love the beauty of the sea. She respects the sea, and she will not go beyond the harbor. The open water chills her, she says, and makes her think of death. Many of her family met their maker by the sea, but that is what comes of living near it, says I.' He paused again. 'She is a rare person Vladimir Baronoffsky has found, a woman so lovely and kind, who can do all a man can and smile through it is a rarity on this earth. She will follow him anywhere, and I would bet she would lead him if the going gets tough. How is it there are not other women like this? Oh, not that I would trade my Meg for another, or change her either, I just see how life could be more complete if we could somehow be partners in things like the Baronoffskys. Perhaps, she would be with me here now and my cold arms would not feel so heavy and empty. Perhaps I could again feel the fullness and warmth of life in the love I remember on our wedding night. Too much time has passed since my Meg has been in my arms, and I am very lonely for her touch.' His voice trailed off.

"Then Mitchell, the tall, thin Englishman, began to talk in his country gentleman's voice. 'Oh, it was like yesterday my lovely Margaret agreed to be my wife. The years, twenty-one of them to be exact, on the morrow have been all too quick to pass. Being a man of the sea, I have spent too much time away, and I shall never get it back. I have been on the sea and far away while each of my three sons came into the world. It takes a strong woman to live the life of a sailor's wife, it does.

She is as pretty today as the day we met in the market at London Square, selling her father's fish. A beauty she was then, and I regret letting her alone for fear someone will grab her up. Young she was, a mere child of thirteen but with all of the beauty of a woman, and today a woman she is. She is warm and loving and hard-working too. She has the fish market where she works with our sons everyday. I love them true, but I cannot leave this life for the turmoil and drudgery of a fish market, harsh as it may be. Maybe I should try to be there with her and set my anchor in the village square. I am afraid of doing it, for I have already been seduced by the sirens of the sea.' He stopped talking and looked over the rail feeling the wind in his face. 'It is good that there is no way back except by the way we came, for I might leave the *Discovery* and begin the trek for the love of her. It has been too long a journey and the sirens may have set me free, for I hear them no longer in the night, only her voice in my sleep. I expect there are no others like Susan Baronoffsky on this earth. It would take someone like her to bear up under the rigors of life at sea. Margaret is a fine and wonderful strong woman but her life will be spent in our village and she will never see beyond the dell, for she is a creature of comfort. I cannot help but think at times how people can know there is a world greater than any man could ever see, and still keep the home fire burning. To me, the flame inside a person goes out when adventure fades from his life. Margaret's flame has never been kindled, but even in her steady way she is the light of my life.' He rocked his head back and looked up the mast through the webbing of stays and lines to see the clouds drifting against the evening sky.

"'These same clouds will blow their way to England, and these same stars are the ones she looks at there in the London night. So even though we are so far apart we share a moment together. Months will pass before I make passage back. I pray God keeps her safe, for though I have left her, I could not bear to go on without her.'

"Roland, the Spaniard, raised his usually quiet voice to

speak to both men from where he was seated against the port side gunwale, his feet folded under him. He was using a marlin spike to out a new eye in the worn end of a topping lift. He was one of the crew who never let himself be idle.

"'I hear you both talking,' he said his loneliness showing through in quick, tense words. He had deep eyes set close together above a generous nose, and a habit of standing directly in front of a person when he spoke. He was shy and not used to talking to more than one person at a time. Here, most of the crew and a few strangers were listening. He raised his eyes to see them all looking toward him. He stopped mid-sentence, looked at the deck, then leaned against the ship. 'I have known you both for many months and many miles. I have known you through storm and calm, hail and the burning sun, but never will I understand how you could gather the strength or stupidity to leave such women behind.' He stopped and took a deep breath that was almost a sigh. Fearing he might have offended them, he smiled, extended his arms toward them as if to send comfort, and went on 'I have waited and searched the continents and oceans for such a woman, whether a Susan, a Meg, or a Margaret. But I have not seen even their tracks in the sand. I can tell you both and all those who will listen, I will make a vow before them and God. I swear should such a woman ever take me for hers, I shall never leave her for the love of the sea.'

"As if in salute to families far away, the player of the concertina began a slow waltz, and sang.

"'There is love in the air,
It has me floating all around
It is catching my heart there,
And finally I am found.

"'Love is in the air, yes love is in the air
It is catching my heart there, it is catching my heart there
You are so far away from me
I want to hurry back to you,

I could swim across the sea
Please say that you will marry me.

"'Love is in the air, yes love is in the air
It is catching my heart there, it is catching my heart there.'

"This brilliant tenor voice rose above the concertina. The native women began to hum in harmony with the instrument, picking up the rhythm and creating an orchestra of voices floating on the wind. Others began to sway to the music. The groom with the bride waltzed slowly at first, then with swoops and circles as the bride bent at the waist to look up and be guided – almost carried – around the mahogany deck. The natives, sailors, and officers were mixed together as if to make up a quilt of understanding.

"Captain Goddard stepped forward proudly at Baronoffsky's eye contact and danced with the bride. Baronoffsky put his arm through the calico sleeve of the matron of honor. With her stubby bowed legs hidden under the calico, and her eyes disappearing in the sun darkened wrinkles of her smile, she seemed to float like a doll in his arms. Someone on the foredeck gathered all of the ship's signal flags and raised them to the tallest mast. The *Discovery* was indeed a thing to behold with its multicolored flags flying high and the music of a hundred voices sending a waltz across the water, as four people now danced and twirled atop the pilot house.

"From their place on the shore, as the lengthening evening shadows crept in with the gray sand of the falling tide, some of the lesser officials of the trade post silently began to wish they had stayed aboard. Music rode in waves to the shore, softened by the wash of the tide and fullness of the evening breeze. They stood well above the beach, and from the hard, naked land they saw the outline of the *Discovery* against the red sunset.

"As the music faded and the twilight overtook the day, the soft light of lanterns cast dancing shadows on the *Discovery*.

There Captain Goddard stood at attention with the officers. In a tight double line below the flags and lanterns, he presented the bride and groom with his personal Bible in which he had inscribed, 'On this 13th day of June, in the year of our Lord 1863, I Francois Louie Goddard, Captain of the auxiliary sailing vessel *Discovery*, stood before these witnesses on the high seas to join together in Holy Matrimony Dr. Vladimir Curi Baronoffsky and Susan Sukaruk.'

"He had entered the names of the ship's officers, and each in turn had signed his name and written a note of best wishes or bible verse to seal the marriage. It would be the Baronoffsky family Bible forever after.

"Captain Goddard had thought through his responsibilities carefully. His friend was now recorded as a doctor not only in the ships logs of the *Sarafin* and *Discovery*, but in his own wedding certificate. In addition, Sukaruk, though she did not fully realize the implications, had been born in a land owned by Russia in a place not even shown on maps of the day. There was no record of her birth, indeed she did not even have a recorded name until one appeared out of Captain Goddard's imagination on the marriage certificate. Now with the certificate suddenly she had more than one new name, and a new husband. She stood in Baronoffsky's arms, relaxed in the slow roll of the *Discovery*, thinking how quickly things change, and wondered how much of Sukaruk there was left but happy with the way she felt. She liked all of these new friends and the way they treated each other.

"Val and Susan Baronoffsky stood on the cabin top and waved goodbye to the departing natives late in the night.

"Susan spoke first. 'I know I am still learning the language and it will be while before I speak as well as you, but now we must talk and there must never be a time when we do not talk.'

"'I know how important that is. I see these men who have left their wives and lovers to explore the sea, so I too have something to say.'

"'What is it?'

"'You say there must never be a time when we do not talk and I agree. But I must tell you I think there should never be a time when we are apart.'

"'Yes, I feel if two people are joined to one, this should be for all the rest of their life. If they part by choice, then they were not really one. I do not understand that way of life and I would not want to be part of it.'

"'It would be a terrible way to live and I do not understand it either. I want our children to be with us both.'

"'Children?'

"'Many loud, healthy beautiful children, all just like you.'

"'Val, I will give you all my love forever. I will give you everything the heavens bless us with and I will love and care for them as I will for you.'

"'We will find our place on this earth where we can have a family and this place will be by the sea. It must be by the sea. We must be able to hear and smell the sea. We must be able to feel the power of the tide.'

"'Yes, the sea.' And she was in his arms, tight against him as the wind ruffled her hair, lifting and wrapping it around his shoulder. As her tresses pulled back from her dusky skin he could see where the hair had shaded her brow from the sun. The skin had a soft whiteness, almost ivory colored. The wind pulled back from her face and showed the delicate sculpture of her cheeks.

"As she nuzzled against the rough uniform coat, pushing the front open with her cheek, she reached her hand inside of his shirt and felt the warmth of his chest, which was hard with a ripple of muscle.

"'I would never think of leaving you behind. I am as sure of this as I am sure I would never let the sun set on any bad feelings which ever might happen to us. Not only will we always travel through life as one person, there will never be a time or place when I will speak ill of you. I will always hold you up in public, no matter what. Understand this, I love you more than life itself.'"

Grandma paused and blinked back the tears from her eyes. I could see that the story meant much to her. I too was touched and I tried to pretend that my emotion was only the pain in my arm and shoulder. She knew though what it was and rubbed her hand over my head, saying, "You will never meet another person who has the kind of heritage you do. You go upstairs and nap now because I need to get dinner. Tomorrow we will talk about the Skid Road."

"What's that?"

"You go dream of the *Sarafin* and the *Discovery*, and tomorrow we will discover a city."

CHAPTER 11

Stump Town's Skid Road

The next day I didn't even say good morning before I asked her to tell me about Skid Road. I heard the screen on the back door bang shut when she came in. I heard her stop for a few moments on the back porch to grab an armful of kindling for the wood box in the kitchen. My job was to keep it full but I didn't feel up to it the day before, and now I felt a little embarrassed she had to do it for me, but she didn't mention it. By the time I hobbled into her kitchen the wood box was full and the stove was flaring up again.

She had returned from the Mission with two shopping bags full of clothes needing to be washed, at least that's what my nose told me. She put the bundles aside.

"No hurry for these old things now," she said. "The old Cap'n passed on last night in his sleep. I'll be making these clean and patched for someone else who will need them in that drafty place this winter. The old Cap'n was quite a man, a real legend around these parts. I'm gonna miss him. Here we are in 1950, and he's gone after being on this earth some eighty five years, born in 1865, died in 1950. What a life he had. When he was born there were no airplanes, cars, telephones, or radios. Must have been quite a different world then, wouldn't you think?"

I tried to imagine what it would be like, but couldn't quite get the picture in my mind. Scenes of the city were too common to me and Seattle was a city where everything was new and modern. I couldn't imagine a city without electricity, cars, buses, trucks, streetlights, electric signs or skyscrapers. I wanted to get her back on track so I asked, "Do you suppose the old Cap'n knew what the Skid Road was?"

"The old Cap'n was born here in Seattle not long after the time your great grandparents settled here. Skid Road, huh?"

I didn't know what it was but I knew it was going to be fun to find out. I felt better, and I was primed for a long session. I made up my mind I was going to keep her talking all day if I could. She began with a poem.

"Behold a city just being born,

Above these ships which wait on tides,

Beneath green slopes with snowy sides,

From which great trees will soon be shorn

Upon emerald slopes above dark waters,

To meet the needs of rich men's daughters,

Above the ships which wait on tides."

I homed in right away on the rich men's daughters part, because all we talked about so far was the Arctic wilderness and the sea. Right away I wondered what being me, had to do with rich men's daughters. She did it again, she had me hooked.

She went on, "In 1863 the steep, heavily forested waterfront of Puget Sound was beginning to give birth to a city that would be called Seattle. Then this was a muddy, backward place with few of the comforts of home, which the settlers had taken for granted before setting foot on the Oregon Trail, and this place beyond trail's end. As little as ten years before in the village of Seattle, there were more Indians than whites, whites numbering only a few hundred in the entire territory. Living here was a pioneer existence, but compared to life on the long Oregon Trail things were good, because this was a place of plenty and of beauty where a person could have roots. Not having to go further down the trail made the pioneer's future look rosier than the life they had known on the wagon trains and river scows.

"Food was easy to gather from the bays and rivers, game was plentiful, weather was mild, and the forests held trees that were like cathedrals. There were the beginnings of other communities on surrounding streams and bays all along the sound, and a constant flow of newcomers from the East by way of the Oregon Trail added other hearty souls to the mix. Of course if asked, all of them had settled at the place where the land was best, and where the city would be biggest. So there was great hope for Olympia, Centralia, Mukilteo, Port Townsend, Port Ludlow, and a host of other settlements each hoping to be the New York of the Oregon and Washington Territories.

"The old Oregon Trail ended at Oregon City, which is just outside of where Portland, Oregon is today. Now you can drive from Oregon City to Seattle on a modern highway in a few hours. In those days, people spent the better part of a year on the Oregon Trail from back East, and when they got to Oregon City, weeks more would pass before they could negotiate the trail to Puget Sound.

"Many of the settlers around Seattle chose to come by boat. They took river scows downstream on the Columbia and Willamette Rivers, then transferred to ships. The ocean trip from the mouth of the great Columbia River to Puget Sound would have to be by stout, ocean-going ships and nothing less. The trip was hazardous by itself and proved to be the greatest challenge for many of them. The mouth of the Columbia River is not called 'the Graveyard of the Pacific' for nothing.

"In the new settlements around Puget Sound there were incredible opportunities for enterprising people, and the hope of finding gold at the end of the rainbow brought many dreamers to the steep, forested hills near where Seattle lies today. But the frontier settlement wasn't heaven – just had the makings, as local supporters would advertise to any newcomer. The long trek on the trail weeded out the weakest and worst prepared in a very systematic way. Some people have said it was only the dumb ones who persisted to the end of the trail, and when they got to Oregon City, the very dumbest would find a farther place to go. Seattle was farther than Oregon City, and had a memorable collection of characters.

"Doc Maynard stands out from the crowd because he was bigger than life in the things he did, perhaps because he did the things others only wished they could. He was not a man who would lie in his death bed and say to himself, 'If only I would have... I wish I would have... Why didn't I....?' His life made its own adventure, and while it was happening people would whisper and gossip, but old Doc gave life, help, and prosperity to more people than were ever hurt by him. Even in hard times he acted like his cup was running over and what spilled out would help another.

"Doc was a real doctor who ran a medical school in Ohio, and was one of those people who could and would do almost anything. So life found him also being a store keeper, farmer, lawyer, fisherman, logger, politician, justice of the peace, a fair blacksmith, a millionaire (at least on paper), and a pauper in debt. His fortunes turned especially bad at the not-tender age of forty-two. One fine Ohio day he bid farewell to his wife, the medical school he ran there, and two grown sons to join a wagon train heading west, bound for the gold fields of California to earn back the fortune he had lost.

"Not a man to be lonely long, he soon became a friendly helper to a young widow on the trail, and by sundown he was driving her wagon, and it was pulling his mule. His good attitude would soon see her as wife number two, even while there was still a wife number one back in Ohio. The good doctor plied his skills along the trail and as the Old West would have it, his doctoring was often free. As only Doc Maynard could do it, he would sometimes leave a gift with the patient. There were plenty of patients along the Oregon Trail, so he arrived at trail's end with less in his pockets than he started with, but a reputation that would have him either as the local entertainment or the local hero depending on whether the story was told at a saloon or quilting bee. If ever there was a man who had no enemies, this was he – discounting of course wife number one, and to a lesser extent fifteen or twenty luckless, formerly well-to-do poker players encountered along the way.

"Crossing the flatiron prairie for Doc was one big game of penny, nickel, dime draw. His life was based on the enjoyment of playing the crummy cards you're dealt and pinning your hopes on better cards to come. Bluffing and getting puffed up when you're short, hanging back when you're fat. Doc didn't do either one consistently and at times he bet his hand without picking up the cards until the call. Cards, like life, was about fun and people for him. Never leaving the table early, he would bet on the last card to fall and end the night with a high stakes winner-take-all cut of the cards. Losing to Doc was like losing to the wind – he never pushed to collect, and he didn't keep score beyond the end of the game.

"At one time he would own, then give away, piece by piece the city of Seattle, and why not – he actually named it, you know. The Indian Chief, for which Seattle is named, was one of Doc's best friends and drinking buddies for many years. The chief drank coffee, and Doc would try to find the bottom of anything with spirits in it. The Chief was always good to have around for safety's sake, being a formidable figure among both whites and Indians. He was always someone with whom Doc could have a good time and not find himself left out in the rain till morning, as some saloon keepers were inclined to do.

"By 1863, Doc had already enjoyed a decade as one of the 'original' founders of Seattle. Ten years before, he had joined with A. Denney, C. Boren, W. Bell, and J. Low to lay claim to the waterfront that would later become the heart of the city. He wandered upon the scene after these other four men had already taken the main claims adjacent to deep water. Doc's personality won out, and the men moved their claims over a bit to make a place on the water for Doc.

"Doc brought with him the contents of a store he had set up earlier in Olympia. Old Doc was the closest thing Seattle could have as doctor, store, and a dozen other things in one package. He also brought Chief Seattle with him. Chief Seattle was the one who urged him to move his store to the new city, and provided the Indian power necessary to do it. Indians moved the store across the water on a scow, with open canoes taking four days to travel the forty or so miles.

"The settlement began to prosper immediately with Doc building a new career as a lumberman. Doc and the others sent pilings, squared timbers, and shingles south to California. Doc, who actually enjoyed cutting wood, operated a wood yard and the Seattle Exchange. When Henry Yesler came through looking for a place to build the first steam powered lumber mill on Puget Sound, Doc gave him prime waterfront land. His neighbor, Boren, was impressed with Doc's good sense and also donated a large parcel, including the top of an area now known as Capital Hill.

"The mill proved to be a gold mine for Yesler if not for all of Seattle. The logs became lumber and the trees became money. The Seattle area was rich with old growth fir, and the mill ran around the clock to fill the orders carried on large ships, which could dock near the mill in the naturally deep harbor.

"Doc became an expert at giving land away to people whom he thought would be a nice addition to the growing city, or selling it for as little as ten or twenty dollars. Soon his original 640 acre claim was a checkerboard owned largely by others. Doc was no better at being a record keeper than a serious businessman, and in time, matters became confused. It became nearly impossible to tell exactly who owned what. By and by, Doc had either given nearly all of the original claim away, or in one way or another lost it to wife number one. She had a good lawyer and Doc was easy to track down.

"As with other settlements on the American frontier there were troubles with the original owners, the Indians, and trouble between the different tribes. Doc had always championed their cause and took the side of his Indian friends when unfriendly tribes came to town. Other whites separated themselves from Indian politics. Among the Indians, there were shooting skirmishes and deaths on both sides, but Doc worked to bring peace and understanding. He supported basic needs of Indian families who might otherwise have acted out their dissatisfaction with the white outsiders if times were too hard for them. They could see settlers eagerly taking their land and ruining the countryside. The whites on the town site he had helped to establish turned away from him because he did not hesitate to treat Indian patients. By 1863, Seattle was a bustling survivor of the Indian wars, but Doc did not share in the riches. He had become almost landless and nearly destitute. Demon Rum and Chief Seattle were his only friends. Doc was proud of the way the city was growing, but he did not own hundreds of acres of it anymore, and in these few years time seemed to have passed him by.

"Hundreds of people now lived in and near the settlement, and there were jobs at the mill and on the waterfront. Timber was king and dozens of men and horses worked to cut the trees to fill the waiting ships. The logs were so huge that they had to be dragged by teams of oxen or horses straining in long lines. The horses would pull and the logs would skid, making the forest floor a quagmire in the year-round rains. Horse paths became grooves in the earth, and the grooves became deeper and wider with the crushing weight of the timber. The Skid Road to the mill became full of traffic year-round, and small businesses began to sprout on either side. Skid Road was the heart of old Seattle. It was the place on the waterfront that people stepping off the steamers and sailing ships would see first. The Skid Road held the commercial center and industry and became home to the bankers, bakers, bums, and whores."

I was only ten but I knew what a whore was, and she knew I knew. I started thinking again about the rich men's daughters and she caught me grinning. She went on, "Seattle, by 1863, was still tiny, though it had become a bustling 24-hour-a-day center of activity. The city was made up mostly of single men since it was still in many ways a frontier, and there was a long hard journey from the East to get there. Still, the city showed some signs of coming greatness. The young city had some fine homes on land donated by Doc, churches on land donated by Doc, a large and busy lumber mill on land donated by Doc, a Masonic Temple on land donated by Doc, and an assortment of businesses also on land donated by Doc. All of this lined the sides of Skid Road, which was also on land donated by Doc.

"The army of hardy men, most of whom worked in the woods or came in as crews from the visiting ships, had few single women to keep them company. Providing female company became a fledgling business. Then almost overnight, it became an industry pushing money circulation round-the-clock.

"The *Discovery* did not sail by a schedule. The Russian American Company and the other trading companies that used the *Discovery* and vessels like her were at the mercy of the weather. As steam powered vessels grew in number, schedules were becoming more common but were realistic only on short coastal trips between major ports. On routes such as the one served by the *Discovery*, a trip into Seattle could happen once every two years or three times a year. The arrivals depended on weather and the cargo. If the ship delivered supplies to all of the posts, and if trading happened to fill the cargo hold for the return, a round trip including Seattle could possibly be made in a matter of months. The *Discovery* was powered by sail and steam so did not have to wait days for a favorable wind as did some of the old fashioned square-rigged sailing ships. Most of the square rigs could expect to see Seattle once a year, unless they got caught in the ice up north and had to winter over. If they survived, the ship could be gone for two years or perhaps longer, as the trade winds defined the route the ship would take.

The *Discovery* usually made every stop where fur trading was a possibility. This meant anchoring offshore to put boats over the side even at small villages without trade posts, and the ceremonial haggling couldn't be rushed. The marriage of Val and Susan was three months old before the *Discovery* dropped anchor at the foot of Skid Road. The leather bound books on the shelf of the Baronoffskys' cabin had been used extensively as teaching material, and when the anchor splashed into the sound, Susan could read aloud from the books and the diary her husband had begun.

"Some of the trade posts, such as the one at New Archangel, in Russian Alaska, now called Sitka, were visited so often and by so many different ships that mail was often left there. Each ship calling there would provide a reliable and free delivery of all letters going the same direction. It was there Baronoffsky left the following letter:

"Honorable, Nikolai Baronoffsky

Number 434, Pavlovski Building

1400 Avenue of the Czars

Kiev, Russia

Dearest Mother and Father,

"I am writing you this letter from my cabin on the good ship Discovery. I am writing midday on 14 June 1863, on the rolling swells of the Bering Sea. We are southbound under full sail on

the Russian American Company trading route. I will be leaving this letter at New Archangel, where we should be calling in a few weeks time. There is much traffic and commerce and I expect this will not be there long before being picked up by a vessel bound for Russia.

"I have not written you since I left San Francisco aboard the Beluga. *I accepted a berth aboard the vessel after working as a doctor in the California gold field and staking a claim there. My companion, Adam, and I did quite well at our mine, and I have a sizeable account in the San Francisco Banks, as does Adam. I am saddened to write that Adam and the* Beluga *met their ends in the Arctic ice. I am the sole survivor of a tragic series of events which I shall recount for you when we are together The adventure Adam and I were attracted to ended in the loss of my friend of four years.*

"I have thought of you and mother often, and am ever grateful for your patient support and encouragement, and the fine upbringing you were able to give me. I, unlike many others I have met along the roads, rivers and oceans I have traveled, am able to meet life straight on as you both taught and I am deeply grateful. From time to time I meet others who traveled through Kiev or are soon to be on their way there and I have used these as opportunities to send mail, which I hope has been delivered. I last heard word of your good health just before leaving San Francisco, having run into Father Georgeff. He was meeting with Trade Company officials to begin setting up missions near New Archangel and recalled meeting with you in Kiev not long before to arrange the legalities of some necessary land claims. Since that meeting, mail from home has not been able to catch up with me, nor as you will understand, have I been in a position to send any to you. I assure you though I am healthy and in many respects happier than I have been in my life.

"I do love and respect you both, and I ask your forgiveness. I have found myself asking for the hand of a lovely lady without

first receiving your counsel. I know you want my happiness and you brought me up to have good judgment so please accept my decision to act on the feelings I felt so strongly and have never felt before. My love for this woman knows no bounds and she will be a wonderful mother to your grandchildren, who promise to be beautiful and strong. I now ask for your blessing, for she now bears the Baronoffsky family name. I have taken her as my wife in a Christian ceremony and I have never felt more strongly that I have done the proper thing.

"I feel at times I love her more than life itself. I can hardly bear to sleep at night for fear of losing her to the darkness. We are as if one in heart and soul. Our thoughts and our dreams are so much alike they are as if we have known each other in another time. I love this woman who makes me feel as if my life is just beginning. She is much younger than I, but among her people marriage to an older man is the usual course of events, and she took me happily. She is seventeen years old, but wise beyond her years. She cannot return to her native village which was wiped out by disease last winter, so we shall make a new life for the both of us in the new city on Puget Sound called Seattle, in the Washington Territory.

"I have heard this new city is in need of a doctor, as the one there now has taken to drink often and is said he can scarcely mind himself. Land in the city can be had quite readily, as people who can add something to the town are often rewarded for staying with gifts of land. So we shall settle there. I shall be a doctor, and dear Father and Mother, I hope very soon that you shall be grandparents.

"So sure am I of my intentions that I now invite you to visit Susan and me, as by the time you arrive in Seattle we shall be comfortably settled and God willing you will be able to meet your grandchild.

"Your Loving Son, Val.

"The *Discovery* arrived on a gray Seattle day with a gentle breeze and a flood tide. There was dampness in the air, though rain had not fallen since the prior day. Against the distant horizon, dark water seemed to hold up the flat bottomed clouds. The city bustle could be seen and heard from the *Discovery*'s berth in the harbor.

"The whistle of Yesler's mill cut the air and steam escaped from every seam. People strode alongside the streets on wooden sidewalks, and wagons hustled to and fro. The Skid Road went straight away from the waterfront, past the mill and up the hill. Huge trees came down the muddy way, dragged by great teams of horses and oxen. Streets next to the Skid Road were used by many wagons and people, but eventually they too would converge along Skid Road, as the greater part of the city was beginning to grow up there. Infant business ventures lined both sides above and below the mill.

"As Baronoffsky looked out over the bowsprit of the *Discovery*, at anchor in the harbor, his eyes scanned the waterfront. He could see far beyond the city and across the bay. Separated from the city, by miles of beach and trees, there was smoke rising from a village peppered with low huts, fleas on a dog's back, he thought. There were canoes pulled up on the gravel and a few people stood next to them. They were far off but he could not make out any horses, wagons, or large buildings. Paths connected the huts and the smoke was coming from small open fires outside. He knew these were the Indian camps, and wondered why they were so far from the main town where there should be opportunities for everyone. Then he remembered Father Ivanoff's trade post and the attitude of the factor and his staff. He wondered if disdain for the natives ran through the fabric of this community here as well. He rationalized that a greater number of whites would surely bring the calm and good sense of civilization to this place.

"He had yet to learn of the ravages that racial hatred had

brought to this new city and the legacy of bigotry that would spread and infect others. The early history of the community was engulfed in fights with the Indians, and deaths on both sides. The local confrontations had been made worse by the seeping overtones of state's rights, the Civil War and slavery, which was tearing the entire country and even families apart. In the North and South, race was an undercurrent that surfaced easily, even if a conflict had other root causes. Seattle was a distant place from the killing fields and hollows, but not so far away that people did not in one way or another take sides.

"There were many Indian tribes near Seattle. Some were friendly, some were not. By 1863, their long history of conflict had made tribal differences irreconcilable. Before the settlers showed up some Indians occupied the town site itself, and in the early years they existed alongside the settlers. By 1863, most of them had taken up residence miles down the beach or across the bay.

"Eight years before, Indians East of the Cascade Mountains less than a hundred miles from Seattle had risen up against the settlers there, and the U.S. Army had been called in. That fall, settlers near Seattle were raided by the Muckleshoots, a tribe that lived some distance south of the white settlement. Several settlers were killed in the skirmish. The Navy war sloop, *Decatur,* was brought in to help, and fired cannons at Indians in hills behind the city while the locals took shelter in a blockhouse. Open hostilities did not continue long and the local Indian population, which was comprised of other tribes, remained friendly during the entire series of events. Still, color lines had been drawn and the wounds were not easily healed. Indians became clearly set apart from the community in their lifestyle, even more than they had been at the time of the fighting. They lived apart from the settlers and as time went on their numbers got smaller and their camps got poorer, as the settlers grew in prosperity and numbers. By 1863 the Indians were minorities, if not outcasts, in this city that bore the name of one of their greatest chiefs. Into this divided community Vladimir Baronoffsky would walk with his young native wife.

"It was common for the men at Yesler's Mill to seek company with Indian women, and several had Indian 'wives.' They were not real marriages and the relationships were usually short lived. Indians lived in their villages and whites lived in their town, or in farms in the countryside. The Indian 'wives' were never escorted through the streets of Seattle, were never expected to socialize with white women, and could never visit their 'husbands' at the mill as some other wives did. Some of the 'real Christian wives' would bring a fresh hot lunch or a cold drink and spend a few minutes of lunchtime in the company of their husbands and friends. The mill was a man's world unto itself, and no women worked there, not even in the kitchen.

"The whites in the community were closely tied because they had a great deal in common. There was very little friction among the whites except squabbling between a few husbands and wives, which everyone took as normal and sometimes entertaining. If a troublemaker came to town, he soon found himself alone and unable to find work. Some were even advised to leave. This solidarity built on a common interest gave outsiders no one with whom to join ranks, and so long as the leadership was benevolent, the town was a healthy place to live for anyone who could fit in so long as they were white.

"Viewed from the bridge of the *Discovery*, Seattle had a clean, well kept face. The buildings were made of excellent lumber and the town had been well laid out. From the harbor, the settlement seemed like an organized place where people took pride in themselves and their lives. A light haze of wood smoke hung in the air from cooking fires. The mill put out great huffs of steam and a pulsating column of black smoke, like a breathing, living thing. The area around Skid Road looked like a hive being served by many insects. The mill seemed to gobble logs as if they were being sacrificed to it.

"Sounds of children came rolling down and across the water with a peal of a bell someplace in a hillside tower. A wagon loaded with barrels and sacks pulled away from the general store, and sound of a concertina drifted from a saloon hidden near the trees down the beach and beyond the road to the mill.

"Above the water, a banner was strung across the dock on the tall posts that held the end of the dock in place. The banner was canvas painted with great red letters proclaiming, 'Seattle, the Biggest Little City in the World.' The letters were too long for the sign and the last two words trailed off and looked as if they were pulling the rest of the banner into the water. Somebody had hung their wash to dry over the top of it.

"There were a few smart looking Victorian homes on the ridge overlooking the commercial center. Three of them were complete with fancy gables, porches, and turrets. Everything on the hillside that had been painted was painted white. The rest of the landscape was green, even where the huge trees had been cut and dragged off. The giant stumps still poked up everywhere. They were impossible to miss because they had been cut off so far above their fat roots that they were as tall as a small house. Waste limbs, bark, and split or rotted logs burned in place, and a blue haze hung under the ever present clouds. Waste from the mill downtown was taken to the mud flats on the waterfront and dumped there.

"There were four ships in the harbor awaiting logs. The logs were tied into rafts then floated to the ships where they would be hoisted one at a time and placed deep within the hold. The rafting and loading operation lasted from dawn to dusk. Even so, the crews from the ships would scurry ashore at dark to follow their ears to music and laughing women.

"Seattle's red light district was separated from the respectable part of town by the mill which took up one side of Skid Road. The mill was on one side, warehouses and the waterfront on another, with scattered houses and steep undeveloped slopes on the rest. From the city's residential area and the business district, it was not possible to see traffic into and out of the area. Indeed one could pass through the mill, skirt a few warehouses, and enter the row of small houses behind the saloon without being seen. The small houses each had a colorful name over a bright painted door, and the ladies who worked there splashed themselves in perfume that drifted on the summer evening air as the night shift went out.

"The prostitutes had come from the California gold fields with not a man among them. They were welcomed by the city fathers as just another industry and a necessary one, whose risk seemed small and the rewards – even if intangible seemed real, if fleeting. The ladies minded their own business and there were no complaints. Local politicians made sure they were registered to vote and took ample time to explain how that was done. The ladies in turn explained how other things were done and the politicians became regular customers.

"All of the whores were young and to a certain measure attractive. Not attractive in the sense of beauty, art, or finesse. But in the sense of desire, which of course, is why they were professionals. Who knows what their real names and stories might have been. They fancied themselves as 'Tiger Woman,' 'Big Red,' 'Lucy Love,' 'Sharing Sharon,' 'Sweet Ginger,' and all the others had only one name except the one called Marie De Paris.

"They all appeared to be in their early twenties except Big Red, whose age no one had the nerve to guess or ask, and Marie De Paris who was the prettiest but who had a sophistication which could only come with age. It was impossible to tell how old she was. Her clear skin had no wrinkles though her hair had a few strands of silver. She spoke as if she were well bred and educated, and carried herself with an air of conservative dignity. She was always more stylishly dressed than the others, in well tailored outfits and expensive but not gaudy jewelry.

"She had arrived in the city with a traveling theatre company. Her dignity, angelic voice and sincere smile endeared her to the crowd that jammed into the lantern lit tent. Before the show started, she met people comfortably and openly, sharing her desire to be a children's music teacher – someday in a place like Seattle. People were friendly and kind, and there was a suggestion that she might receive a free lot as such gifts were standard for new and desirable businesses. Delighted with prospects of a future, she had her trunk taken off the ship that afternoon.

"During the evening show, a stagehand mining pockets in the crowd got caught with his hand around the wallet of a bear-sized, ham-fisted logger. A short fight erupted and the entire theatre company was run out of town – less Marie, of course, who was momentarily accepted as mentor for Seattle's young people interested in learning about the performing arts. The battered pickpocket was convinced that Marie had turned him in, and got even by spreading the news about her past. The women who had gushed about wanting her to stay stopped speaking to her, and it became clear there would be no gift of a lot on which to build the music school – and the promised extra room at the house on the hill vanished. She was stranded in Seattle, friendless, humiliated, and depressed as the theatre company left without her. Late in the day, she was welcomed by Big Red and introduced to the ladies that worked in the cabins behind the Mad House Saloon.

"It was Big Red, though, who was a favorite of sailors, and the tougher they were the better she liked them. She had a sailing ship tattooed on her stomach, and anchors on the front of each thigh. The ship crashed through the waves under full sail. The tattoo was old and faded, but still a much talked about work of art. She was a coarse woman who laughed with almost with every breath, and could remember every off-color story ever told, and could embellish to make them even better. She may have been a beautiful young lady once, but her face, now weathered and wrinkled, would take on a comic appearance whenever she laughed. Even in the noise and commotion of a Saturday night she often could be heard yelling, 'Shiver me timbers Laddie, trim me sails,' and her laughter would start in a low chuckle. She would get louder and start yelling, 'Weigh me anchors, Laddie, weigh me anchors,' then the laugh would get louder as she would scream, 'Fire the cannon, Laddie, fire the cannon.' It was not uncommon for her to have a line of tattooed sailors at her front door, or waiting for her at the Mad House Saloon when the ships came in. The rest of the girls called her Mom.

"Marie De Paris seemed as though she would be more at home in the best Boston society. She was impeccable in her appearance and had the largest and best wardrobe of anyone in Seattle. She preferred white gowns with lacy fronts with narrow waists, and a few had tiny flowers embroidered in white on the bodice. She loved to talk of Paris and the theater. On Sunday nights she would sometimes tell tales of the opera to the other ladies, who were captivated by the story. Even when she was with her men she would wear expensive rubies, sapphires, diamonds, and gold chains. She had more jewelry than all of the rest of Seattle, and most was fit for European royalty.

"Marie De Paris would find herself at the center of the ladies' Sunday night gatherings, as if something depending on her had been prearranged.

"'Tell us about the opera,' someone would say.

"And she began, 'I think Paris is the world capital of opera. Not only do many composers of eminence live there, but even those living there do not feel they have arrived until they have had a Paris success. Even during the Revolution, opera was not put aside. Indeed, the Revolution gave composers cause to strengthen the plot, for times were very disturbed and hair's breadth escapes through the loyalty of friends or servants happened often. There was much danger and violence in Paris, and some of the operas I have told you about exploit danger and suspense, complete with a thrilling last-minute rescue. The good characters are full of sentiment, love, understanding, loyalty and kindness. Possibly, this could happen to any of us.'

"Each Sunday she would tell the story of a different opera, unless someone had a special request, which was never. She went on. 'Tonight I will tell you of an opera set in a different time and place. This opera which is called Muette was written by a Frenchman named Auber who had a talent for light, pretty music. His story is based on an actual historical event, the revolution at Naples in 1647. It, too, is a time and place of revolution. In the opera the revolution is led by Masaniello, a fisherman. In many ways this is a violent opera because it culminates in the eruption of Mt. Vesuvius, which was also a real event, though in 1631, but still a fitting and grand climax.

"'This opera is so filled with passion that when shown at Brussels in August of 1830, it began the popular uprising which led to a new Constitution of Belgium as an independent state by the following year.' None of the girls knew where Belgium was but they didn't interrupt.

"'This opera is much different also in that the heroine is a mute. She expresses herself only in pantomime, in accompaniment of the orchestra. The music is filled with choruses, crowd scenes, processions, ballets and a huge finale. But there are some light and fun parts such as the marketplace scene sung by fun loving people like ourselves.' The girls looked at each other and exchanged smiles and nudging of elbows. 'But this is a serious opera and the mood in song often rises from romantic to patriotic, and some of the duets sound as if they were being sung to the accompaniment of a military band, like this one, for example.' She hummed a passage as the girls picked it up, humming in the background, she sang a few of the words. She stopped to describe in great detail the costumes, the stage, and how the actors played their parts.

"Then she went back to the beginning to describe the elegance of the theater and where the best places were, who might be there that night, and where she would sit. She would describe the box and the flowers sent by secret admirers. She would describe the carriage in which she would be delivered, and the fine cottage in which she lived with the cozy garden in back.

"The girls gathered on Sundays to talk and sing. Their voices could be heard up the hill in the middle of the day as families sat down to their Sunday dinner and the mill was quiet. One of the ladies had a clear, bright voice that climbed above background voices and sounds of the wind in the trees. Sometimes she would sing 'Amazing Grace,' and old Doc Maynard alone in his store would cry. All of them were white."

CHAPTER 12

The Dream

He stood a long time near the bow of the *Discovery* looking out over the bowsprit's carved figurehead, wondering of the many places this fine ship and its remarkable crew had visited. He felt as if they were family, but he knew now was the time to start his own.

"There was scarcely a breeze and the giant firs above the settlement were still in the morning light. The smell of wood smoke rose from chimneys in light blue tufts that floated above the hill. People and wagons moved in the town and the shake roofed mill's machinery could be heard above the swish of waves against the hull.

"The mill looked alive within a cloud of steam, and the smoke that belched in a great dark plume from the boiler. Everything near the unpainted mill's walls was covered with a wood dust and layers of soot from the steam engine. A man with a wheelbarrow was moving a pile of sawdust nearly as large as the mill itself. The mound was growing faster than he could wheel it to the waterfront to dump on the mud of the bay. A train of logs was being dragged on skids down the central road, which was full of horses and oxen traveling in both directions. Some people stood close to each other in a tight circle and talked on the board walkway near the largest store.

"The other streets of the city were quieter than Skid Road.

There were a variety of houses scattered around the hillside, and from somewhere, the bell sent out its measured chime. From the dock children's voices carried across the water. The children were all about eight or ten years old. There were seven of them, one was a girl with blond pigtails. Two were dark-skinned and shoeless. The two dark-skinned boys had a bucket full of fish which they were sharing with the others by putting them on strings to be taken home. Five of the children skipped off, heading up the hill of Skid Road while the two darker ones settled back into their fishing at the end of the dock in the shadow of the waving sign.

"The homes were white with shake roofs. They were neat homes and some even had picket fences. There was an absence of log houses, perhaps because the mill made cut lumber so convenient. Above the town, and on the edge of the trees, four Victorian homes stood, complete with fancy gables and porches. The largest one reflected a stray beam of sunlight off a rain-wet facade. Two of the homes had widow walks on their roofs and all four had tall turrets looking out over the bay. There was a flagpole in front of one with a ship's yardarm flying an assortment of colorful flags. The sun had not risen high enough in the sky to remove the shadow off the tree line, and the town just faded into the trees.

"The officers and men of the *Discovery* took leave in Seattle, going ashore in boats. The welcome banner had come loose from the piling, and dragged one end in the water. Two boys had left their fishing poles against the pier to tug and pull the end of the heavy wet canvas sign onto the dock. When they had pulled the banner in, they did not know what to do next, so they folded it on the dock with one end still tied high above. It now read, The Biggest Little.

"As the officer's skiff drifted up to the pier, the two dark-skinned boys hurried over and pulled them in. They held the skiff steady as everyone stepped onto the ladder that covered the distance between the tide level and the top of the pier. One of the officers had tucked a pair of embroidered white gloves too loosely into the broad waistband of his coat. As he stood to reach for the ladder, the gloves fell into the water and began to sink under the weight of the silver chain that decorated the wrist opening. Immediately the running tide began to move the gloves out of reach as they continued to sink in the glass clear water, glittering like shiny fish. Both of the boys jumped into the water head-first without a word and disappeared below the surface in a swelling cloud of bubbles. Moments later they surfaced, each one with a glove in an outstretched hand.

"The boys held the gloves out to the richly dressed officers as if the gloves were treasures. The officers pulled the boys onto the dock and warmed them with their coats. Then they rowed back to the *Discovery* with the boys wrapped in the officers' finest clothing, fed them a hot meal and gave each boy a wool blanket for his own, then took them back ashore. Back on the dock, the smallest of the two, a boy about eight years old, stopped and rubbed the mud off of the boots of the man who had dropped the gloves. There were no words spoken, and as the man reached out to pat the youngster on the head, the boys were already out of reach running and skipping down the alley with their willow branch fishing poles and bucket of fish. They ran off toward the Indian camp at the outskirts of town.

"Seattle had become a popular retirement place for seamen. The busy waterfront offered a place to see the ships coming and going, and to them this meant keeping in touch with old friends. The city had magnificent marine views, good recreational sailing, and outstanding fishing. It was a cheap place to settle and stay, unlike California and the cities of the East Coast, and land was readily available at the town center. For seafaring men, this was a paradise.

"Ships calling at Seattle often stayed a few days so the officers and crews had time to visit. On this day, the officers went en mass to visit the retired captain of the *Sarafin,* who had settled in Seattle years before. He had a built one of the Victorian mansions above the city and equipped the center of the front yard with a mast and yardarm. He had imported paint in a variety of bright colors and trimmed the house and its fancy shingles and spindles. His was the most colorful house in the city, and perhaps in the Washington Territory, not counting the row of buildings behind the Mad House Saloon. Without the flags and colorful paint the house would have taken on the air of a lonely old maid. It was perhaps the finest house in the Washington Territory.

"The captain of the *Sarafin* saw the officers arrival through his telescope, which was set up near a ship's wheel in his bay window. By the time they were halfway up the hill he had glasses ready, and a bar set up atop a curved oak buffet that had been sent over from England. A fire crackled in the open fireplace and orange shadows glittered and danced off the French doors between the parlor and dining room. The windows were large for a Victorian. The drapes were subdued floral material with an under layer of lace trimmed in silk to soften the light but still leave the rooms bright on gray days.

"Except for the officers, the rest of the men of the *Discovery* went en masse to visit the Mad House Saloon and the girls they knew worked there and in the little cabins out back. The boys from the crew stayed a long time at the saloon, being sure to be fair and even in the time they spent with each of the girls. The crew of another ship was in town, and they too had permission to stay on shore overnight. As usually happened, there were too few girls to go around and the lines at the back rooms of the Mad House Saloon and in front of Big Red's little cabin were getting longer and longer.

"Near dawn Big Red looked out the cabin door to see two men still waiting. She grabbed both of them and pulled them inside before they could move away. As she did this, someone else squeezed out of the cabin behind her and jumped off the porch in the dark. There was a splash and cussing as he landed in the rain barrel, one leg in and one leg out. She yelled at him, 'Better not come back until you get that fixed.' He disappeared into the dark doubled over in a knock-kneed stagger, heading toward the mill, which was about to signal the morning shift. The tipped over rain barrel rolled down the hill after him as Big Red slammed the cabin door and the bolt rammed home in the lock. The man was still in earshot when she laughed inside the dark cabin and four shoes hit the floor.

"Through good planning and dedication to duty, the crew figured that overall, they needed to be sure each of the girls got at least two visits, but as things worked out most of them got visited several times. Since there were more boys than girls, it took some figuring to ensure that each girl had exactly at least two visits from the boys in the crew of the *Discovery*, and each of the boys had spent exactly what he could afford. Everyone was happy and tired when the sun came up and they all resolved to meet again soon. A few of the drunker ones said a tearful goodbye amid attempts to propose marriage. Big Red would have said yes, but she was not asked.

"Marie De Paris did not participate in the party, and had not been included in the arithmetic. She was cast of a different sort of metal than the rest. She had principles which were all her own and they were not fully understandable, but the other ladies liked her for her differences. They were aware she was a Jew, for she had told them. They were not sure just exactly a Jew was, but a couple of them thought it might be fun and asked to join.

"Nor did Marie De Paris attempt to hide that she was a kept woman, and for a time a lady of the Paris streets. But now, even though beautiful and full of life she seemed to do well without male company in her bed. She thought perhaps the years were catching up with her. The shades were drawn tight in her cabin the entire night the crew of *Discovery* was in town. Invisible from the street, a candelabra burned and reflected off a silver Star of David that cast shimmering light against her ceiling. She spent the night alone and there was a single empty wineglass on the bedside table. On the shelf above her bed was a religious book and beside that, a picture of her parents. Her father wore a simple dark suit with a plain, broad-brimmed hat. He had a full beard and sideburns that fell in front of his shoulders like braids. It was an old photo of such poor quality that her mother was hard to recognize, as if the photographer was not able to place both of them in the light.

"As she slept on the feather bed, her nightgown and jewelry seemed out of place in the cabin's rough sawn walls. Beside her on the bed was a book, *Stories of the Opera*. It was open and her hand relaxed on the page she had been reading as she began to sleep and dream. She dreamed herself into the story.

"As her body felt the warmth and heaviness of a deep sleep, she began to hear orchestra music and see herself in a small French city, standing in the village square facing the open doors of a church. Behind her in the dream are several shops and the center one is that of Eleazar, the goldsmith.

"There is singing coming from the church. One of the worshippers sees activity in the goldsmith's shop across the square from the church, and remarks, 'That Jew is working again on a Christian day.'

"Others in the congregation join in the complaints and insults, and began to sing,

"'Oh you Jewish, this is not your day,
Oh you Jewish, you must go away,
This is not a place for you,'

"'Or any other Jew,' Eleazar says as he glares at them from the door of his shop. In the dream, Marie De Paris runs to him and urges him to go inside. She sings.

"'Father, Father, please, please, turn away, turn away,
This is just another day, let us not be cast away.
I like this place and I will find my love,
I feel the will of God above.'

"It is the year 1414 in the dream, and the emperor has just defeated heretic John Huss and his many followers. He has sent a messenger to the town square to announce the victory and unite Christians under a single faith. The Christians in the church begin to celebrate the victory, dancing and drinking wine in the church and the town square.

"As the party grows late, hammering is heard coming from the shop of Eleazar the Goldsmith. The crowd circles the shop and pelts the front with stones, demanding to know who would dare work during a Christian celebration of victory over the heretics. Eleazar and Marie come forward into the square and announce in song,

"'We are the children of God,
We are victorious,
We are righteous,
We are children of God.'

"The messenger, now standing on the steps of the church, hears the activity in the square and orders Eleazar and Marie arrested. Eleazar vehemently denounces all Christians as heretics, and Christianity as a false religion. The messenger orders Eleazar and Marie put to death by boiling them alive, singing,

"'It is time to end the evil within you
Christians shall be the ones which bring you
To your silent salvation beyond this place.
We the Christians know your race.'

"As they are marched under guard to the top of a wooden platform above an iron cauldron surrounded by a screaming mob, a man walks to the front of the crowd. He is dressed in a red cape with the imperial crest emblazoned on the front and rear of the cape. The crowd parts for him. He wears a silver helmet and silk clothing. The crowd becomes quiet. He stands and gazes at the beauty of Marie, mesmerized. He sings to her from his place at the front of the crowd,

"'Marry me, my love, and I shall be with you forever.
I love you now and I always shall.
Be my Christian wife.
I swear, I shall leave you never,
I can now hear the silver bell,
I know that this will save your life.'

"She realizes she cannot give up her faith for any earthly reason and cries out in song,

"'I love you, I love you, I love you.
I have waited for you here,
I could feel you coming near,
But I will always be a Jew,
And always loving you.
My heart has always been for thee,
But now my God waits, near for me.'

"Eleazar throws up his hands and sings, 'Praise God, Praise God, Praise God.' He clasps his arms around his daughter and in tears, both of them jump together into the boiling water. In the dream she sees the scene from above as the pot boils. She sees her eyes become white and the skin peel from her bones. The crowd sings a chorus,

"'Let them be food for the swine,
Let them stop heresy for all time,
Let them be as worms in the ground,
Now for them God has been found.'

"Then the soldier climbs the platform above the boiling pot, and facing the crowd, sings with a breaking voice,

"'You are the evil in this world of lies, and hate,
Open your eyes, you have sealed your fate,
You are all one, with the evil beast,
Of all men, you are among the least.'

"The crowd closes in on him and from within the mob there is the silver flash of a dagger. The crowd parts and the soldiers body is spread upon the platform. A bloody gash runs from his heart across his chest and stomach to his groin. The faces in the mob turn black; the people begin to burn. The mob turns into a crackling fire. There is thunder and lightning.

"With a start, Marie De Paris awoke wet with cold perspiration. She sat on the edge of the mattress with her head cradled in her arms. The white nightgown and bed covers flowed around her like a robe. She shivered and choked as she could not keep back tears. She had experienced this dream many times since leaving Paris. In the last few years it became increasingly frequent. She felt she was going insane.

"She dipped a cloth in the wash basin and wiped her face. As she did, she parted the curtain and raised the blind slightly.

"The sun was rising and the horizon softened with a streak of yellow and red. The colors reflected off the bay. In the harbor, a man and woman stood shoulder to shoulder on the deck of a new arrival, the mast mirrored in the calm as if a finger pointing the way. Birds chirped, and up the hill a rooster crowed. She could hear the boiler at the mill began to vent steam as the morning shift stoked the fire. It was like life was beginning all over again for someone.

She sat down and removed the wash basin from the stand. She retrieved a piece of light blue paper scented with roses, with tiny roses in each corner. With her jeweled pen she began to print in small capital letters:

"TO WHOM IT MAY CONCERN. THIS IS THE LAST WILL AND TESTAMENT OF THE LADY KNOWN HERE AS MARIE DE PARIS WHO BEING OF TROUBLED SOUL WISHES TO END HER DAYS ON THIS EARTH AT HER OWN HAND. MY UNHAPPINESS IS THE RESPONSIBILITY OF NO ONE BUT MYSELF. I HAD MANY CHOICES DURING MY 41 YEARS AND FEW IF ANY DO I REGRET. I KNOW IT IS NOT POSSIBLE TO GO BACK AND RELIVE ONE'S LIFE, AND AM NOT SURE I WOULD IF I COULD. THERE HAVE BEEN MOMENTS OF GREAT HAPPINESS AND TRUE LOVE. I LOST BOTH MANY YEARS AGO, AND IT WAS THEN LIVING CAME TO AN END, FOR THAT IS WHEN I LOST MY HEART.

"I CAME HERE TO START LIFE ANEW AND FAILED. I AM GRATEFUL FOR THE MANY FRIENDS HERE AND WISH TO REMEMBER THEM IN THIS WILL. I BEQUEATH MY RINGS TO THE OTHER LADIES WHO SHARE THE SMALL CABINS NEXT TO MINE AND I ASK HERE THAT MY FRIEND BIG RED DISTRIBUTE MY RINGS AMONG THEM AS FAIRLY AS POSSIBLE. TO HER I LEAVE MY RUBY PIN AND SOLITAIRE DIAMOND PENDANT.

"IN THE STRONGBOX BENEATH MY BED THERE ARE A NUMBER OF GOLD CHAINS AND A BOX OF GOLD COINS. I WISH FOR THEM TO BE GIVEN AS A GIFT TO THE NEXT DOCTOR WHO MAKES A HOME HERE. HE MAY USE THE INHERITANCE TO

BENEFIT HIS PRACTICE ANY WAY HE DESIRES. THE LOOSE DIAMONDS IN THE STRONGBOX ARE TO BE SENT TO MY SISTER IN PARIS. SHE IS REBA STEINHAUSE GOLDBERG. SHE LIVES IN THE REAR OF HER DRESS SHOP AT 421 RUE DE LA CRUX. THE COINS BESIDE ME ARE TO BE USED FOR A HEADSTONE IN THE GRAVEYARD HERE. THE STONE SHOULD READ GOLDA STEINHAUSE, 1822 – 1863; SHE HAD ILL WILL FOR NONE AND BEST REGARDS FOR ALL. PLEASE SET THE STONE IN THE MORNING SUN. I WISH FOR MY BODY TO BE BURIED AT SEA SO PLEASE TAKE ME TO THE PLACE WHERE THE STRAIT MEETS THE OCEAN AND CAST ME OVERBOARD. FORGIVE ME FOR LEAVING YOU THIS WAY. GOLDA MARIE STEINHAUSE.

"She than sharpened her razor on a leather strap. Standing in the flickering light she quickly drank two glasses of red wine, then sat on the edge of the bed as she slit one wrist, then changed hands, and barely able to grip the razor, slit the other. Blood gushed forth. She became lightheaded and lay back on the bed. The blood ran onto the floor and followed the path of the grooves in the boards. The rivulets ran to the door and under it, dripping onto the front stoop. She was dead before the sun rose over Skid Road.

"While Val and Susan Baronoffsky enjoyed the quiet and solitude aboard the *Discovery*, word of their arrival spread throughout the townspeople. It did not take long for the city to learn that the talented new doctor and his new wife planned to make Seattle home.

"The ship's crew had bragged about his talent, but it was the girls who made up the Bedpost Bulletin that spread word to the mill workers. The mill workers, of course, told the lumberjacks, and the lumberjacks told the farmers. The politicians learned firsthand during their usual encounters with the girls. The businessmen, of course, heard last from their customers who usually came into the stores and shops as a family. Before Baronoffsky had met a Seattle resident, he could already boast a powerful reputation. The word had gotten around to everyone but the late Marie De Paris.

CHAPTER 13

Coming Home

She did it again. What started as a little talk with Grandma became a real long story, but I was excited. I slept in late the next day, so I must have been getting better, but I still hurt all over. I took pride in my pain because so many people thought I should have been killed. A few grownups came by from time to time to see how I was mending. I felt kind of important even though the ones who were most amazed at how tough I was always ended their assessment with, "Boy, how stupid."

My friends came by to see how I was doing, and they brought a kitten for me. I didn't want it, but Grandma got attached to the slightly crossed eyes right away. When my friend Bonnie put the kitten down on the kitchen floor, it tried to climb into Grandma's chair. The kitten was too small to make it by herself and fell back to the floor, landing on her back and looking goofy in the process. I never saw a cat fall without landing on all four feet. Then the kitten walked over to where Grandma left her shoes to dry next to the old stove. The kitten climbed into one of the worn black shoes and looked around like she was driving a car. When Grandma named her Hydromatic, Hydro for short, I knew I had a kitten whether I wanted one or not.

Grandma said, "Any kitten that smooth and shiftless has to

be named Hydromatic." She began to warm a little milk on the stove, and I was hoping she would not get so interested in Hydromatic that I would not get to hear the rest of the story.

Bonnie said with me laid up the baseball team didn't have anyone who could throw the ball fast enough to scare the opposing batters. They all tried it, and the batters were getting hit in the back and feet. Our team forfeited the first two games in the second inning because the score was so one-sided. She said the team probably wouldn't win any games so instead of trying to play baseball all the time, we would all be going berry picking at Bainbridge Island soon. She had talked her father into driving us to the ferry terminal at 5:00 a.m.

The farmers would be waiting at the terminal on the island side in their old trucks. I imagined new trucks, or trucks all one color, weren't allowed around the berry farms. For some reason they all had seats with the springs sticking out and beds with the tailgates broken off or hanging down. None of them had fenders that were smooth and round. The trucks rattled and banged and slid their way around the dirt and gravel roads but most of the farms were not far from the ferry, so the rides were usually exciting but short.

The farmers hired pickers at the terminal on the island, then drove them to the farms for the whole day. Anyone who got off the ferry could have a job if they wanted one. It wasn't like playing ball where sometimes you had to stand around and be embarrassed by being the last one picked. The farmers treated all of the kids as if they had already made the team and the little ones really liked that.

There would always be the same mix of people waiting to be given a ride to the farms. The crowd would be about half kids, mixed evenly between boys and girls, most of them white. And then there would be the older folks, mostly older ladies with faded scarves and worn, brimmed hats. The women always had stained fingers from the berries, even before work started in the early morning, and their clothing seemed to be made for a larger person. When they stood talking in the field, their loose coats and shirts fluttered, making the farm look like a field of scarecrows in red gloves.

The ladies were Filipino and Japanese, and even though the farmers preferred them, the farmers had some kind of agreement to share them equally. So no matter what truck you got into, the seat inside would be taken by an older lady, and the places where you could sit in the bed with your back up against the window would also be occupied by them. The old ladies talked constantly in their native language, so the only thing you could make out would be "crazy" or sometimes "wow" and "funny huh?" Some of us kids rode in the back of the bed, shoulder to shoulder, feet dangling out of the open tail gate.

It was back-breaking work in the muddy fields all day long, and I really did not want to do it ever again. I told her I would love to go but I was still hurting a lot.

Some of us went berry picking the year before. That morning I was up so early I felt like I hadn't gone to bed. I wondered if I had even gotten to sleep, because when I got up I didn't even have to pee and I wasn't hungry. We walked to the bus stop in the dark and waited a long time in the drizzle. In my hurry I left my jacket and lunch sack in the house and had to stand in the drizzle again halfway through the trip, waiting for the transfer bus to the ferry terminal. Both busses were chilly and my clothes were wet all the way through when I got on the first one. The windows were fogged over, so as we rattled and splashed along in the dark it was like we weren't really moving. Some people napped with their heads against the shaking glass, as a blurry halo of lights moved past in the dark outside. I was shivering and sleepy by the time we got to the ferry dock, and by then I was getting hungry. I was starved, almost lightheaded, when we got to the fields and right away I started eating the berries. I ate a lot of them and the farmer got a little upset because I was still eating when people started turning in their flats to get them checked.

By mid morning the sun was out and my clothing was almost dry but my stomach was hurting. Like lightening I had to go to the bathroom, but there was just a stinky outhouse. It really stunk, even though the walls had so many cracks you could see out of them if you put your face up close. From inside, I saw people working and talking. Some of them were looking at the outhouse as though they might come over. I had shut the door and twisted the piece of wood that served as a latch, and kept one hand on the door. At first I tried to hold my breath, but I couldn't. Just as I sat down next to the Sears and Roebuck catalogue I took a big gulp of air and felt sick. One of the kids from the berry picking bus walked by and hit the side of the outhouse with a board and I felt as if the whole flimsy thing was going to fall into the hole. I got so tense I couldn't go.

I went outside and started to feel sicker. Some of the people might have felt sorry for me when I threw up, but a few seemed to get mad. The event happened at the well pump where everyone drank. It was bright red and got all over the front of my shirt. So here I was sick, very tired, smelling bad, constipated, miles from home and it was starting to rain again.

This particular farmer had a daughter. She was about a year or so older than I, eleven maybe, but looking much older. She took pity on me and led me up to the house. She was pretty and very nice. She had blue eyes and long blond hair. Her family had lived on the island for many years. The family farm was an old homestead her great-grandfather had established when he came to the Washington Territory after the Civil War. He had fought in it, she said. She went to school on the island and had only been off once.

She loved being there, and I wondered how she could, but then I soon learned they had a real toilet inside the house. The one out in the field was for the help so the house wouldn't get all dirty. When I heard it flush and her father walked down the hall and out the front door, I knew my stomach cramps would soon be relieved.

I asked her if I could wash my shirt in the bathroom sink. She said she could run the washer for me, but I countered it wouldn't be right for me to have some of my clothing off if her father or someone else came in. I don't think she knew what I meant.

It was a handsome sight – the throne there in the gleaming white bathroom surrounded with a tile floor. Everything smelled new and clean. I ripped off my shirt and let it settle into the sink as I opened the faucets. I wrestled my pants down and sat on the toilet. What an incredible relief. Then after a moment I couldn't stop going. I started to wish I had opened the window, but it was out of reach. I reached for the paper and there was only cardboard left on the roll. I got off the pot to shut off the faucet when the sink started to run over and looked to see if there was any more paper under the sink. There was not, so I did what I thought at the time was the wise thing to do, since I had been in the bathroom too long already. My new friend called from down the hall, "Everything okay, you all right, do you want me to wash it for you?" I figured I would use one of their washcloths to wipe myself and just flush everything down the toilet. Then I would wring out my shirt, and everything would be fine. I wondered if other people got into these kinds of messes but just did not talk about them.

So I carried out my plan. Just before I flushed the toilet I thought, gee that looks awful full. But I was committed. I flushed and right away it started to fill up. The water came up to the rim in a boiling, swirling mass. It looked like it was going to stop, but then began to splash onto the tile. The mess covered the floor and started to flow toward the door and I panicked. I made a dam out of the bath towel and stopped the flow right at the bottom of the door and started to mop frantically with the other towels. Everything was a mess and I had no choice but to wring the towels out in the tub. I turned on the shower to wash everything down the drain. When I stood up and turned to look at the mess the window caught my eye. I did not wait around to try to explain any of this. I let myself out the window with my wet but nearly clean shirt and walked through the woods behind the house to the road, being careful to move quickly and stay low.

I hitched with the first car I saw and the woman drove me all the way to the ferry. She was a nice gray-haired lady driving a Chrysler sedan with wide whitewall tires and fog lights. It was black, and to me smelled new, but after my morning almost everything smelled new. The lady did not ask a lot of questions, and when she got me there, she gave me lunch money and a ferry ticket. The lunch money was all I had to show for the whole day.

I had to wait at the ferry terminal for my friends because I knew they wouldn't leave if they thought I was still on the island. There was no way to leave a message, and for certain I was not going back to the farm. I told my friends I rode with someone else to the ferry when they finally did arrive, and the only lie I told was when everyone was comparing how much money they made.

The ferry boats thumped and hummed all of the time. The faster they went the more the decks and windows vibrated. They had high-backed benches, and some of the benches faced each other, with a table between them. We all sat at one of these. The boats were always clean and freshly painted. Actually, if you looked close you could see that there was so much paint used to keep out the effects of sea water, that sometimes they painted over the important things. The machinery that would have to be used to lower the life boats was covered with so much paint that the cranks and pulleys appeared to be useless unless they had an ax to chop the paint off. The rules were no rust allowed, no matter what.

I rested my head against one of the large windows. The engine throbbed deep inside the hull, a heartbeat giving life to the giant propellers that churned up the salt water. The sky was gray all the way down to the water, the same drab, cold, lifeless, color. Far away a few sailboats lay on their sides beating their way back to warm living rooms in the city, I thought. All I saw was the tips of their sails, almost as if they were trying not to sail off the edge of a flat world. I was happy to be coming home. I felt as if I had been on a very long journey.

So when Bonnie brought up the idea of berry picking I used my arm as an excuse. I was glad she asked me, though, because the invitation meant she had not heard about my adventure last summer, and I was surprised that her dad, Giuseppe, tolerated me enough to allow me in his new car.

He was a little funny about the new car. Always talking about Italy – I used to wonder why he bought a new Chevrolet if Italian stuff was so great. I heard the mailman call Giuseppe Gus once, and he got real loud and acted insulted yelling stuff down the sidewalk in Italian, then waving his arms over his head. He stomped his heels sort of like in the movies about Mussolini and Hitler. He was very proud of anything Italian.

Just after he got the Chevy, I was showing some of the other kids how to play slide down the fender. I thought Giuseppe was at work even though this was Saturday. Giuseppe saw me through the kitchen window and came flying out the door screaming about scratches on the paint, called me a dumb Indian, and ran me off. The next day on the way to school I stuffed a couple of potatoes up the tail pipe. I walked by on the way home and the car was still in the driveway, but now his new Chevy was being hooked up to a tow truck. Jeez, I was glad I didn't tell anyone about the potatoes. I didn't want the car to break down, just maybe make it smell not quite so new for good old Giuseppe. For some reason it picked that day to not start. The guys at the garage found the potatoes before Giuseppe had a chance to get it started and warmed up.

He worked in a wine distributing company, less than a block from the Fiat dealership. The guy who owned the place was Jewish, and his kid Mort played on our baseball team, too. Mort was the only kid with a catcher's mitt and he had to be there or we couldn't use it. Mort was a hall monitor and crossing guard. He kept what he called *the secret list of violators*. I wondered how could it be secret if he kept telling me I was on it? Mort used to say Giuseppe's family were gangsters, and that made Bonnie cry. When I told him to be quiet he said he was going to punch me in the nose, so I hit him in the stomach and he keeled over. I hated myself because I thought both families were crooks, but she was my best friend.

Even a ten-year-old knows people are as different as day and night, but nobody seems to know for sure what makes them that way or how to change them back. Us kids used to play on the broken old cars abandoned in the rear of the Andy Martin's Mobile station out by the old Rainier ballpark in the summer, and Andy never seemed to mind. He was just a nice old guy with a big smile my dad liked to shoot the breeze with. For a guy who ran a gas station and crawled under cars, he always had a shiny black necktie and a clean, sun-bright, crinkly stiff, uniform shirt. Even late in the day his uniform was cleaner than the ball players strutting, scratching, and spiting below the cheering crowd across the street. I never saw anybody cheer for Andy, but he had more friends than anybody, my Dad said.

We parked the car there on ballgame nights and sometimes they would get to talking and laughing so much we missed part of the game, but me and my friends didn't care. The station was at the foot of Beacon Hill, which rose steeply behind it like a rumpled green blanket. There were hardly any houses on the slope back then, and the rear of the station, thick with old cars, seemed to be at the edge of a wilderness. The front was different though. The station opened its paved driveways to busy Rainier Avenue, and shared the intersection with a supermarket, the ballpark parking lots and grandstands, and a drive-in restaurant with real car hops and flashy hot rods. On ball game nights the intersection was brightly lit, so you could see the whole world going by, and Andy seemed to know everybody. When the beat up yellow trolleys glided up and rattled to a stop out front, even the drivers would lean forward and give him a sort of salute, the way he saluted customers when they drove up to the pumps, just as he was greeting them by name. I saw it happen a lot.

"Hi Andy. Would you gas her up please?"

"Yes sir, Mr. Chatalis. How is Mrs. Chatalis and the two boys?" He listened, washing the windshield from the driver's side as the gas ran in. He went on, "I understand Bill is off to the U of W next fall. I was talking with Mr. Fortune, his calculus teacher at Franklin yesterday, and he says Bill is clearly the best student. You must be proud of those boys, especially after such a great year in football. I am proud to know them. I filled their Chevy last night when they came by at eleven. They were with Paul Lewis and Pat Brennan, just on the way home after a dance at Roosevelt. Good sons with good solid friends. Can't beat that." For Andy, customers became family and their kids didn't have a chance of getting away with anything.

When my Dad was killed just before the end of the war, Andy came to the house the day we heard, and stayed a long time. He didn't know what to say, so he sort of stood quietly letting people in and out of the front door, looking strong and friendly in a neat, new looking, double breasted black suit and new shoes. He had to explain to some people who he was, extending his hard square hand, fingernails clean and trimmed, saying, "'I'm Andy, and these folks are my friends, have been ever since I can remember. I help them celebrate birthdays, cheer at the ball games, fix a tire or two." His kind calming smile came through a clean shaven weathered face with deep wrinkles.

For years after my Dad was killed, Andy arrived at the house for a short visit every six months or so. He picked up Mom's car and left another. A few hours later he returned it shiny and clean from tires to top and he wouldn't let my Mom pay for anything. When things were dark for us he provided just enough light, but that was just Andy being Andy.

Bonnie's Dad never said a thing to us at the house when my father died. They were supposed to be neighbors, and friends, but all he did was stop his car out front and holler out the window to ask me if I was going to move away to the reservation now.

He was in the car with his two brothers, Frank and Joe Carbozello. Joe was the older and larger of the two. He had a sharp nose and slicked back hair, in addition to the hair that grew out of his nose and ears. Like bear fur the hair curled up out of his collar all the way around his neck, and he had one large eyebrow. He had tattoos on both hands that disappeared up the sleeves of the denim work shirts he always wore. He also wore a white cap pulled down too tight around his head so his ears stuck out. The hat was plated with union buttons. He was a union organizer, and bragged to everyone, even us kids, that he was friends with Dave Beck, Jimmy Hoffa, and Harry Bridges.

Frank was the youngest of the three, but he was the smartest. He was a nicer dresser and drove a cleaner car. People said he was probably the honest one in the family. He hardly ever came to visit at Bonnie's house, but when he did, he spent most of the time talking to Bonnie's Mom while Joe and Giuseppe drank in the darkened garage behind the house.

Joe was usually dirty and smelled of rotten vegetables. His car was almost brand new, but with broken windows. The inside was littered with papers, cigarette butts, and dirty clothes. Sometimes, it was hard to tell the difference between Joe and Bonnie's Dad, Giuseppe. Nothing about them looked good in the light of day.

By the time Grandma and Hydro got settled down the day was well underway. I figured this next part of the story would be shorter now that she had something else to occupy her. As she prepared lunch for us, she started talking.

She said, "Do you realize your great grandpa became somewhat of a hero and outcast all in one swoop just as soon as he came to town? The whites had disdain for the Indians on the outskirts of town and did not care to keep track of what conditions were like in their camps.

"The morning Val and Susan Baronoffsky rowed themselves to the city dock from the *Discovery*, for their first visit to the city, the water was near dead calm under a cloudless sky.

Gulls sat on the water. Two Indian boys sat on the end of the dock and grabbed the boat as it came in. They stared at Susan. She looked like one of them but she dressed in clean tailored garments. She smelled like roses and her fingernails were not cracked and dirty. When she smiled at them, her white teeth were even and bright.

"Her eyes sparkled as she looked at them and said, 'Thank you. My name is Susan. What is your name?'

"'People in our village call us by our Indian names, but we want to be called Tom and Robert.'

"'Tom and Robert it will be, then.'

"'Where is the place you live?' asked Val.

"Robert pointed south toward the head of the bay. 'Tom and I don't like to be there because too many people are sick and some are dying. We have our blankets and we sleep over by the mill. When rain pours we sleep under the lumber pile. We fish here and sometimes we cook on our own fire. When the tide is out we can get clams and sell them to the ladies up the hill.' He pointed to the line of white houses at the far end of Skid Road. 'They feed us sometimes.' Robert was doing all the talking while Tom looked at his feet and wiggled his toes.

"Robert and Tom appeared to be healthy and confident. They were dressed only in tattered pants, in the morning chill but the day was warming and they would probably be quite comfortable. It was still early morning, and though they did not shiver, both boys had goosebumps. Their bucket was nearly full of fish.

"Baronoffsky asked them if they would show them this place where the people were becoming sick. The boys walked quickly and tirelessly around the buildings and past the mill, heading towards the head of the bay. They led the way behind the warehouses and down the alley where the cabins with bright painted doors were. There was activity on one of the porches. As they came closer they could hear the conversation. Most of the people were prostitutes, and they were crying.

"But the two boys led the way past the cabins, along the

mud flats of the shoreline and through the woods. Part of the way the trail was fit for a wagon, but then became a footpath. They walked in single file, weaving their way upwards through a thicket of blackberries, which opened to a meadow whose grass grew as tall as the boys. From their vantage point, they could see the cleared off hillside and mud trails where the ancient forest had been dragged off one log at a time. From above, the giant stumps looked like grave markers in a poorly planned cemetery.

"At the top of the meadow they circled around and began to follow a stream for about a mile. Then they crossed through a stand of cedar trees to crest another hill, from which they could see the Indian village. There was plenty of land all around, but the village was tightly packed, just a few steps between the huts. There was a slow moving tidal stream running through it, the grassy bottom waving in the ebbing current. Some dugout canoes were pulled up on the gray beach. A central cooking fire burned in the middle of the circle of cedar huts. Some children played tag around a group of others sitting and kneeling on the beach near the canoes, while three women worked near the fire. There was no one else around. As the boys approached, the smells of smoked fish and cooked clams rose from the village, and they saw a number of fresh graves just at the edge of the stand of cedars. Three scruffy dogs, tails wagging, ran to the boys. The women stepped towards the boys then hugged them as the boys, the women and the dogs, became almost indistinguishable as others appeared and closed them in. They talked excitedly.

"Everyone else was either sick, dead, or like Robert and Tom, keeping away. The Baronoffskys were offered food and sat on the ground to talk with the others at the fire. Then they examined the sick people, and Val nodded knowingly. He and Susan excused themselves politely, then set out to follow the stream toward the source. Not far above the village, he came to a settler who had begun to build a cabin for his family. Their outhouse stood on the stream bank, and cattle milled around the water. It had not occurred to the Indians that this could be a problem – after living in the wilds for hundreds of years, they had encountered a pollution problem for the first time.

"Later that day the Baronoffskys returned to the village with shovels and began digging a well. The well would be near the stream but away from and higher than any other improvements. Val and Susan instructed the Indians in the importance of boiling their drinking water until the well was done, and spent the night caring for the seriously ill. In the morning, they delivered a shovel to the settlers who were unaware of the problem they had caused. The settlers immediately began to build a new outhouse and fill in the old one, and began a corral for the cattle and a fence to keep them out of the stream.

"It was Robert and Tom, then next the settler, who spread the word that Vladimir Baronoffsky saved the village. The news was met with some ho-hums in the town, especially among those families involved in the skirmishes with the Indians a decade ago. There was even a handful of people who insisted that the judge keep the dead woman's endowment from the new doctor, since he started his practice on the Indians instead of the whites. The disgruntlement only gathered steam when the word got out that Mrs. Susan Baronoffsky was a native herself.

"But just as quickly as it began, it fizzled momentarily after her first public appearance with old Doc Maynard in a clean shirt. Doc may not have been trusted anymore with everyone's health, but he still got a lot of respect as a legend of sorts. At one time or another, he had owned most of the city. That by itself did not scare anyone, but he was such a poor record keeper that he could not prove to any court's satisfaction just exactly what he had given to whom. So everyone who had property in the new city harbored fear Doc might remember, and some of them would immediately be deemed squatters on Doc's property.

"So when old Doc Maynard walked down the Skid Road

boardwalk, past the big church on Sunday, hand in hand with Susan, everyone who owned property in Seattle tipped hats, nodded, and smiled. This included every business owner, worker, politician, and even the local ministers and the girls who worked at the Mad House Saloon. Val and Susan went from being hated to being loved, or at least the appearance of both, in a matter of days.

"So you see Hecky, my father and mother, your great grandparents, were a lot like the tide themselves. They were the same way to everyone just like the tide is. The tide will do what it does, go where it wants – it will treat everyone the same. They had the strength of many oceans. Nothing could bring them down, nothing. They had principles, and would sacrifice them for nothing. Friends loved them for what they were, caring, intelligent people. Your great grandpa was a hell of a doctor."

I was starting to feel a lot better about myself when she told these stories. She said I looked a lot like her dad except I was what she called "chunky." I think she meant fat, but that was okay. I was proud to be compared to him, and as she sent me off for a bath, I was already wondering what turn the story would take next.

CHAPTER 14

The Light of Day

The next morning when I woke, I noticed my arm didn't hurt in the cast anymore, but itched instead. Most of my scrapes were scabbed over and the swelling around my eyes was turning from black to yellow. I could see much better now and I could move around without looking like the walking dead. I had been cooped up in the house for days and it was time to see the world again.

My room was situated at the top of the old house in sort of an attic with a turret at the gable end, close up under the roof. I liked to sit in the window and wait for the evening. I could watch the sunsets and loved when the light softened and the sky started to pull up its covers for the night. Colors of everything outside changed. Not just got darker, but actually changed. The gulls would begin their journey to their overnight nesting places, and the closer it got to dark, the harder and more frantically they hurried back.

Not everyone appreciated dusk the same way though. Bonnie didn't. Once when we kids had a picnic in the backyard with lanterns and everything, she started to cry. There was a magnificent sunset that evening, with clouds that flamed their colors all the way across the sky. Bonnie always saw it, even on a cloudy night. Sometimes she would clasp her arms in front of her and sort of rock. You could barely hear her hum a song she made up as the colors would change. She never whimpered or sobbed, and you wouldn't even know the kind of thing she was feeling unless you looked at her, but I knew we felt the same.

On the sunrise side of the attic there was a little round window, and from it, you could see a hillside about six blocks from the house, and on the hillside was a green expanse – the lawn of a rest home. There were a few old people among the residents, but most were men who had a bad time in the war and who did not have families to help them get along afterward. Some were crippled from terrible diseases they could do nothing about. Some were blind, and others were injured in ways that made them depend on help, even if they looked healthy. In the summer Bonnie and I would walk by there on our way to Volunteer Park. The grass in front of the place would be full of these people sitting in lawn chairs in white bathrobes, or just standing in one spot, sort of waving back and forth. They were so out of touch, most of them acted as if they were alone in an empty room. Some were blind, and they were all so quiet.

On a nice day, orderlies put the people out in the sun like houseplants. They were only outdoors during the day, never the morning or evening, so they missed the changes of the colors. I felt sorry for them because they might have forgotten it was ever there.

The people parked on the grass must have felt every day as I had felt the first day after my head-first tree descent. For a startlingly long time I had not known who I was or where I was. The next day I hurt so much all over that I cried a lot. If they felt like that all the time, they needed help. That's when I decided to do something about it.

In the morning Bonnie came over to visit Hydro, who was doing fine and had taken up residence between Grandma's wood box and the cupboard under the sink. This new residence was the result of Grandma's coaching, and the path the mice used to run in and out of the house. She didn't like to trap them because there was no way to get them without hurting them. She nailed their holes shut and put cheese outside for them, but that only attracted more mice. She pinned her hopes on Hydro.

The three of us sat in the kitchen – four counting Hydro – and I kept talking about how nice the day was and how much I liked to walk. I kept hinting about how good my shoes felt and how my scabs needed some sun. The idea was taking a long time to take hold, so I finally I had to just stand up and say, "Be right back, going for a walk." I stepped out the door real quickly and from the front steps where Bonnie could see me, I started waving and jumping around to get her outside. She had a hard time getting up because Grandma was starting to talk, and sat down right in front of Bonnie. I waved harder and harder. Finally, when Grandma turned toward the stove, Bonnie slid out the door, and my plan was underway.

Bonnie's dad, Giuseppe, was an old country Italian. He and his two younger brothers frequently jawed about the "Old Country" around the big kitchen table with pride, jug of wine between them. All three looked the same – moustaches, big noses, and bellies that hung over their belts just enough to make you wonder what their belt buckles looked like, or if they were even really there. Frank was the one with a clean shirt.

On the Fourth of July, Joe and Giuseppe would climb up to the roof, almost too drunk to hang onto the ladder, and hoist up the wine jug. After dark when the fireworks began to appear around the city, they shot off their shotguns. Somehow they never shot each other.

When the three of them got together they usually invited a bunch of other relatives, too. Theirs was a very large family when all the cousins and in-laws showed up. The men stuck together, taking over the kitchen, laughing, and speaking Italian while they cooked large pots of pasta. They always had lots of bread, sausage and wine in different colors and sizes of jugs. The more wine they drank the louder they got. Eventually one of them would break out the concertina. Then the men danced and everybody sang louder, and louder, and louder.

Neither Bonnie nor I could understand them and neither could her Mom. She was from Seattle, Ballard actually, where all of the rest of the Scandinavians lived. When the brothers came over, Bonnie's mom became real meek. She had to stay out of the kitchen and when they were gone she was expected to clean-up the mess. The drunker the brothers got, the more they expected from her. It would all start with her not being allowed in the "men's kitchen," but later when they needed help to get the table cleaned or more wine they called, "Woman, Woman." They wanted her to know exactly what they wanted, and they wanted it now. She walked among them with her head down, saying nothing. I used to feel sorry for her, but she said, "This is the way the Italian women are and they tell me this is what you do if you are a good wife." And the brothers would say "Yes, yes, that is the way it is supposed to be for a good wife."

Giuseppe made good money as a wine distributor and he seemed to like what he was doing. One day I noticed, quite by accident, he had a habit of bringing his work home with him. Just before my record-breaking tree descent, we were practicing baseball in the street by Bonnie's house. The street was quiet and the lots on both sides were deep, which left plenty of room to set up the bases. We couldn't hit the ball far enough to put anything in danger, so the neighbors let us have our fun. The backstop for the catcher was the side of Giuseppe's garage. They only painted the front and the side you could see from the house and street, and the rest was just rough wooden planks. Wild pitches didn't show marks on the wall. There was a small window on our side of the garage but it was at the far end.

I liked to hit the ball real high, so I used to take a great big swing. The bat we had was a full size Louisville Slugger we got from the broken throwaways at Rainier Ballpark. The handle wasn't broken all the way through, but a cracked bat was no good there. We took it home and I taped it together with electrical tape. The full size bat was too big and heavy for us to swing so I cut about six inches off the handle. When I cut the handle off I also had to cut off the wood flange that kept the bat from flying out of your hands. I think that's why the bat got away from me and went through the window at the end of the garage.

Bonnie was upset, but I calmed her down when I explained you couldn't see the broken window from the street or the house. I was relieved when it didn't dawn on her that Giuseppe would be able to see the problem from the inside of the garage. I wasn't worried, though, because the glass was so dirty the cardboard that I was going to put in wouldn't look any different than the glass, anyway. When I sneaked inside to pick up the broken glass and get the bat, that's when I saw the treasure. The garage was loaded with wooden crates and cardboard boxes of wine bottles and jugs, and they were all full. He had them stacked so high there was a wooden step ladder leaning against the pile. The largest boxes were on the bottom, cardboard crates full of big jugs. The top of the pile was saved for smaller wooden boxes, full of bottles with labels, mostly in Italian.

When Bonnie slipped out the kitchen door, leaving Grandma behind, we went around the house to get my wagon and set out for Giuseppe's garage. She thought we were just going for a walk so she came along and skipped ahead. She looked at me a little strange when I turned the corner for her house but didn't say anything. When I started across her neighbor's yard toward back of the garage, she held back, so we sat down on the wagon and I started to talk to her about the people in the bathrobes at the rest home.

I told her that they were missing the sunrise, the sound of the wind in the trees, the sight of birds in flight, the smell of new flowers, and most of all the sunset. It was as if they were already dead because they had forgotten the world around them. Some of them were hurt in the war and now were condemned to a living graveyard. The rest of the world was alive and new things were being born every minute just as fresh and new as the sun that comes up every morning to make a new day. Sometimes, I got up early just to see the sun break open the night. I wanted them to know life still happened everyday, just like the birds still flew everyday, and the sun still set everyday – life went on. It was easy to make her feel sad for them, and by the time I got to the part about the sunset she was on her feet and moving toward the broken window. We were going to do something good.

When we got to the back of Giuseppe's garage, I pulled out the cardboard pane I'd used to repair the window and swung the window open on its hinge. With my cast on I couldn't pull myself through, so I climbed on the wagon while she kept it from rolling away. There was no wagon on the inside, so I tumbled onto the dirt floor. Enough light came in through the open window to locate the largest cardboard crates. Of course they had the biggest jugs, except they were on the bottom of the pile. I thought I would use my pocket knife to cut the side of a box open and slip out a big jug or two. It took quite a while to remove one of the sides with the little knife, and when I finally got it off I found the weight of all the boxes and crates above was smashing the jugs in place. I couldn't budge them with just one hand and the cast kept me from using the other one.

There was an electrical cord hanging from the socket on the ceiling and I jerked it loose. I cut the end off and threaded the cord through the finger hole on one of the jugs. The other end of the cord went around my waist, leaving about three coils of slack laying on the ground to give me time to get up some speed. I took off for the front of the garage and in about two and one half steps the cord tightened up and one of the jugs bounced sideways out of the box, spinning across the dirt floor. I handed the first jug through the window to Bonnie and she put it on the wagon.

If I would have quit at that point, everything would have been fine, but I tied the cord through another jug handle in the same carton. I ran for the door and the cord tightened up, this time sending me sprawling. The jug was jammed in tight, but it had budged a little. I tried it again and the jug popped out of the carton. I chased it down, took off the cord, then handed the second jug out the window.

I had to get the ladder to climb out of the garage, and as I turned to reached for it, I noticed the whole stack of crates and boxes beginning to lean. The top of the stack was still moving as I climbed out. When I put the cardboard pane back in Giuseppe's window the stack of boxes was leaning even more. As we pulled the wagon with two gallons of wine across the neighbor's yard something behind us crashed. It sounded like breaking glass coming from inside the garage. We started to walk a little faster.

Before we got to the sidewalk I took off my shirt and wrapped it around the wine jugs and put my hat over the top of them. There I was, walking along with no shirt, a cast, two black eyes, numerous scrapes and bruises, pulling a wagon with two jugs of wine hidden beneath my shirt and baseball cap, trying to act normal. Cars drove by and slowed down to take a second look. We had to stop once to chase my hat when a gust of wind from a passing truck blew it off the jugs.

When we got to the grassy area outside the rest home, the people in the bathrobes were already outside standing or sitting in their usual spots, as if they knew no other place. We pulled the wagon over to the center of the bunch, but nobody moved. Some of them couldn't move their arms at all, and others just didn't care. We went into the building and got all of the paper cups that were in the dispenser at the water fountain and took them back out to the wagon.

When I uncovered the jugs one old guy in a wheel chair looked suddenly awake and his lips started to quiver. He watched the jugs carefully, almost lovingly as I slipped my shirt on, and others began to turn and notice the miracle too. Some of them tried to move their chairs across the grass to be closer to the wagon, but couldn't – still they kept trying. They started to help each other, and inch by inch the circle got tighter. As I bent over and opened one jug the smell of wine cut the awful, powdery smell of a rest home. The two blind guys noticed it, too, and turned their heads. Now I had an audience.

I said, "Everyone who wants some of this leave your hands down." I thought that was fair since some of them couldn't raise their hands anyway.

I couldn't handle the heavy jug with just one good arm, and spilled a little as I started to fill cups and hand them out. As the wine splashed into the bottom of the wagon a quiet moan and gasp went up in unison. The two blind guys reached forward and steadied my hands, then they took over. The two blind guys volunteered to be the bartenders. They were the strongest people there and didn't spill a drop.

The people started to talk to each other and called us the Captain and Wonder Woman. They told us their names and where they were from, and drank a toast to us. When Bonnie asked the one who called himself General Foster if they would drink to the sunset, he said, "Why Miss Wonder Woman we would be most proud to honor your wishes."

The blind men filled everybody's cups. Then the woman with no legs, Tillie raised her cup to Bonnie and said, "Thanks to God for all the sunsets, for the beauty painted in the sky and in the mountains. Thanks to God for the colors and the shadows and the songs of sunsets, and God bless you."

They thanked over and over as they poured the Captain and Wonder Woman each a cupful, and we all drank to "the young people of the world." Then they poured us each another cupful and we all drank to peace on earth, then it was all gone.

One of the orderlies started out the door toward the grass where we were gathered. The group turned as one person and waved him back. Even the blind men acted like they knew he was coming down, and they waved too. The orderly stopped for a moment, then lit a cigarette. He began to mosey back to the door. He stopped outside to puff on his cigarette. The people in the white robes were talking to each other and they started to help each other back up the long slope of the sidewalk.

Bonnie and I collected all of the empty paper cups and put them in the wagon with the empty jugs. We dragged everything to the garbage can, then shuffled over to the flower bed, where we sat down out of sight, dizzy, and feeling tired. We both fell asleep among the flowers and butterflies, listening to feeble voices singing God Bless America inside the rest home.

When I woke up the sun had traveled well across the sky. We had been asleep probably for three or four hours. I had a headache and was thirsty. I woke Bonnie up but she was too dizzy to walk, so I pulled her home in the wagon. We were both a little sick, but when she looked at me I could tell she was feeling full and happy inside, like me.

I felt those people who didn't even care who they were or what was going on around them had come back into the world for a moment, at least long enough to see there is a world alive around them. I hoped they would want to see the next sunrise and that they would enjoy it together and talk about it.

I took Bonnie home and helped her onto the porch swing. The clouds were already showing silver streaks all across the horizon. The mountains on the other side of the bay were almost a silhouette against the sky. I put a pillow behind her head and she rested heavily against it. We looked at each other and she touched my hand as she said, "Today was a good day, and we did a very good thing. Thank you. I think those people at the rest home are more alive today then yesterday. I never want to be so sick and sad I cannot see the world around me. There are too many things to see, and feel, and do. I could never be so sick that I couldn't feel the sunset. Thank you for taking me with you today." She closed her eyes and as I walked down the steps I could see the tears starting to come down her face.

"Yes", I said, "We did a very good thing."

When I was pulling the empty wagon around the corner by my house Giuseppe drove by in his new Chevrolet. I waved and hollered, "God bless America." He squealed his tires and just kept on going.

CHAPTER 15

The Piano

I was dead tired when I got home and only wanted to head for my room. I felt worse than I had that morning; my stomach felt sick, my skull hurt, and my body ached. When I rounded the last corner I could see the house. It was beautiful in the shadows of the madrona trees and cedars.

I could hear a woman's voice and she sounded a bit edgy. I couldn't see Grandma yet. There was a white moving van backing over the curb toward the house. The guy driving had a white hat like the one Joe Carbozello wore but it wasn't pulled down over his ears. He had union buttons though. The truck was creeping back real slow and was still creeping back when I saw one of the huge tires start to crunch my grandma's rose bush, which she had planted just weeks before. We yelled at the same time. I screamed, "Stop, stop, no!" She appeared on the porch and said in an even, low voice, "Godamit, you idiot." For some reason I thought she was talking to me, but by that time I was almost to the truck I could tell it was meant for the driver, and so could he.

He chomped down on a stubby wet cigar and cords in his neck stiffened, veins standing out. His face changed color, and just when I thought he was going to come flying out the door of the cab he focused on the big side view mirror and saw her there on the porch. He sort of sunk down into his seat, turned off the engine, then climbed slowly down, leaving the cigar butt behind. He knew what he had done because he had to walk right by the rose petals sticking out from between the dual tires on the back of the truck. He had his hands in front of him like he was saying a prayer as he approached the front porch with tiny little steps. Before he said anything he stood by the remains of the rose bush, removed his cap with both hands and held it over his heart. He was very large and muscular and his face looked too old for his body. I would have guessed him to be almost as old as Grandma.

I couldn't see her but I heard her say from the porch, "It takes some kind of asshole to run over a lady's roses." She said it quietly, but by then he was in front of me looking at the rose petal sticking out from the space between the tires, and we both heard it.

My mouth opened because this was my grandma talking. I saw his was open, too, but for a different reason. He peeked around the rear of the truck and saw her maybe as I did, with the evening light dancing across her thin, strong figure there on the porch, framed by wisteria vines. Her dress moved in the breeze which caught her silver hair and pushed it back from her face to show her olive skin. She stood straight as he approached the bottom stair of the porch. The light caught her eyes and the gray in them sparkled like starlight.

He checked again to make sure he had gotten rid of the wet cigar and was now trying to tuck in his shirt and hold his hat at the same time. His thick hands were plain and clean. The top of his shirt was unbuttoned and a Saint Christopher's medal showed itself laying against his chest on a short gold chain. He stood at the bottom of the porch steps and said nothing. I think he was waiting to be bawled out, and knew he had it coming.

Grandma looked at him, stepped toward him a half step and said, "You always this way?" I could see a trace of a smile on her face. "Ma'am, I am so sorry. I just don't know what to say exactly. I hope you will believe me, when I tell you how sorry I am. I know I have damaged your property because I was careless, but I really did not mean any harm. I have killed your rose bush for sure, I know. Can you forgive me for what I have done? I love roses and all kinds of flowers. I try to keep fresh flowers from my garden in the house all summer. To me they are all beautiful and this is a terrible thing to ruin them this way. I try very hard to grow roses each year and have many plants I love to take care of. This truck is my living. It and others like it, and a long time ago teams of horses served me well hauling pianos and other things for the good people of Seattle for almost half a century. I think I am being a victim of my age, for I did not see your rose there, and I feel like such a sorry old man. I promise you, I will put one of my own roses in place, and I will not move your piano or enter your house until you are satisfied that I am capable and trustworthy."

By the time he was done talking Grandma had her hands up in front of her face like a schoolgirl. She tried to look amused but her eyes were alive with excitement. Her usually strong voice was quivering as she put her hands down to fold her arms loosely in front.

"Oh, let's not make a big deal of it. Life is too short you know. Its just that the piano that you're going to take, has a story to tell. I am not upset over the rose bush – I can grow another, and enjoy doing it. It's the piano that has me out of sorts. How would you like to bury the hatchet?"

"You owe me no apology. I have upset you late in the day when perhaps I should not even be working. I have to admit I grow more tired toward the end of these long days. I do not like to go home to an empty house so I probably bother people too long. My son was killed in the war and the following year my wife of thirty years passed away. I miss them always, but most when I am at home, but even so I still love to tend the garden there. I could never leave the old house and I guess maybe that is sort of the way you feel about the piano. Perhaps I should just come back another time."

"Yes, you can move the piano later, but right now you're getting a lemonade. I am going to tell you about the piano, and you are going to tell me about your son, your wife, your garden and the old house." She reached to grab him by the arm.

She pulled him along toward the kitchen, "My name is Susan. Susan is the same name my mother had. I too lost a son in the war, and a husband after many years of marriage." She waved him across the porch and into the kitchen which smelled of fresh baked bread. She pulled out a chair for him and set a glass of fresh squeezed lemonade on the table.

The glass was frosty with clear rivulets beginning to find their way down the fluted side. Tiny drops came together magnificently in the waning rays of sunlight which still crept into the kitchen, silvering the beveled edges of the tiny diamond shaped panes. His huge hand on the glass, the other one under it, he looked down into the whirlpool that pivoted on his palm. He thought, *It was so good being a tiny bubble at the center of it all. Enjoy the moment now Adrian, for you can't go back.*

She looked toward him as her finger tips held her wet sparkling glass. She was reminded of the sea, and she saw him through the glass as he began to talk.

"Susan, would you please call me Adrian? Atlas Movers is on the truck but I am no Atlas. Adrian is the name my mother gave me after her father. My son put the sign on the truck so I think it will stay there and I will be proud of it."

"Adrian, I like you."

"Sometimes I spend too much time with the memories." He picked Hydro up and she stretched out over his leg, all four feet hanging down.

Outside, in the gathering darkness, one wheel of the truck was steadily sinking into the grass and the other had obliterated the rose bush, but nobody cared. It was after midnight when Adrian excused himself. As he was leaving Grandma asked him to stop by for breakfast. He smiled and pinned one of the union buttons from his hat onto her dress front.

When I got up the next morning the smell of breakfast was heavy in the air. There was more clattering than usual coming from the kitchen. Grandma was singing with the radio as she cleaned off an extra setting. The radio was tuned to a country station that was just ending a Hank Snow song, *I'm Movin' On*. The disc jockey said he was going to play the other Hank, and Hank Williams came on singing *Hey, Good Lookin'*. She looked over at Adrian, who was drinking coffee at the table. He pulled a chair out for me, nodded, and clicked his tongue.

"What about the piano?" I said.

"What do you mean?" Grandma said.

"Would you please tell me the story about the piano?"

"Yes. I would like to do that very much. Knowing about the piano will help you understand who you are. So sit down and get comfortable." They smiled at each other as the song ended, then she turned the radio off.

"That old piano is like a living member of this family even though it doesn't get played anymore. That has been with us through life, death, feast and famine. Did you know the beautiful old thing came here all the way from Germany? Well, it did, by way of Boston and San Francisco, and all for free. That was the only one of eleven others to survive the trip. You see, it was perhaps the first piano in the city of Seattle, and would have been one of the first twelve, but the others got thrown overboard. The auxiliary steamer that they were on, *California Dream*, lost her boiler coming through a tide rip at Point No Point in a gale. The captain had to lighten the deck load to keep the vessel from foundering. He had the crew put up the small main sail, but the wind gusts and rough water heeled the boat over so far it was close to capsizing. They were hauling a cargo of beer below and pianos on deck, so threw over the pianos. When they made a safe moorage the people expecting pianos asked where they were. The captain led them through an exaggerated story of the narrow escape. When asked why he didn't have the beer thrown overboard instead, his reply was, 'Well you can't drink a piano.'

"Eleven of the pianos sank like anchors right away, but this one stayed afloat. It got caught in a whirlpool then it popped free and the current swept it ashore as *California Dream* was clearing the point southbound. It stood in the sand and pebbles of the outgoing tide, miles away to the south, near Apple Cove Point. Your Great Grandpa Baronoffsky came around the point in a sloop on a return trip from Port Gamble, where he had amputated the leg of a logger. He saw the piano sitting there, high and dry, where the tide had left it. It was a beautiful thing even all wet and with the seaweed hanging off it, and out of curiosity he put his small boat ashore. From the beach he gathered together some driftwood logs and stuffed them under the legs so the piano would straddle them. The tide would float the logs up against the piano bottom. He tied them in place, then he tied the odd piano-log raft to the stern of the sloop and waited for the tide to re-float it all. On favorable winds, the strange flotilla made it safely to Seattle many hours later.

"A few days after he got the piano back to Seattle, he took over the old blacksmith shop behind the Mad House Saloon and built a stage at one end. The blacksmith had moved to a place where there was more room to store wagons and a place to corral the horses. When he moved, he built a house next to his new business and left the old shop empty. The old shop was well worn and crudely made, having been originally built by old Doc Maynard, who gave it away to the first blacksmith that happened by, so that he would stay. The blacksmith in turn gave the shop building to young Doc Baronoffsky. Baronoffsky made a sign that said 'Golda Steinhause Seattle Opera House,' and put benches side to side in front of the new stage.

"The gift Golda Steinhause left for the doctor was under her real name, and Baronoffsky had heard that his benefactor was a fan of the opera. He wanted her to be remembered even though he had never met her, at least so he thought. All he knew at the time was that she made it possible for him to begin a practice without any worries about money.

"The Seattle Ladies Club took charge of decorating the

new opera house. They strung decorations from the rafters and fashioned a false curtain to trim the stage, as there was not enough affordable fabric to make an entire curtain. The shop was dark because the blacksmith had always worked by the light of the forge. When the benches were installed, the forge was moved to the rear of the building as a heat source, defeating the purpose as a light source. This was alright so long as the footlights were in service, but without them the room was pitch black inside. The ladies solved the problem by installing kerosene lamps in the rafters. They were raised and lowered on ropes that ran over the rafters then down the wall where they were tied off about waist high to pegs driven into the cedar walls.

"They had forgotten cedar swells with the rain, so when the rains eventually stopped and the huge forge was lit to heat the hall during the first public viewing, the pegs worked loose. The lanterns crashed to the floor and burning kerosene splashed the walls. The place went up in a crackling, popping, column of embers. The double doors of the old smithy had been left on the building at the rear of the stage to make management of scenery easier. Doc Baronoffsky was just down the street when he heard the cries of fire. He ran to the opera house only to see the walls and roof already aflame. He forced open the double doors and there was the piano surrounded by flame but still standing alone in the center of the stage. He tied a rope around one leg and everyone pulled. The piano came to the edge of the stage platform, and just as they were going to allow it to tumble off, the stage collapsed, and the piano rolled down the incline and into the street. They pulled it a few more feet into Skid Road and watched the new opera house burn to the ground.

"The owner of the Mad House Saloon offered to buy the piano. He said, 'The Saloon is the next best place for the piano since everyone would see it there eventually anyway, and you don't have to put on an opera to use it. The girls would really like some good piano music to fill out their cultural experiences. Besides they know more about opera than anyone in town, anyway.' Baronoffsky suspected that the saloon keeper was pulling his leg.

"'If I really believed your girls were fans of the opera I would have named the new opera house after one of them.' The saloon keeper didn't quite know what to make of this. He thought it was some kind of a joke and he too laughed, then everyone gathered in the street joined in.

"Later Baronoffsky asked for the piano to be stored in the empty house with the bright painted door and windows. The saloon keeper said that would be OK. The little cabin was empty except for a few pictures on the wall. While the piano was being moved in, Baronoffsky looked after an injury outside of the burning building. The burns were not serious, as only her outer layers of clothing had burned, but much of her hair had been singed off. She looked very different, especially with swelling getting started on her face. He needed to stay with her to give the reassurance she would need when she looked into the mirror.

"It was not until the next morning, that Baronoffsky went by himself to see that the piano had been properly taken care of. He let himself into the little cabin and stepped into the simple room. There was a fancy iron bed against one wall and the piano against the other. The two things filled the space. Sunlight danced on the yellow walls refracted through glass prisms hanging from the painted glass shade of the overhead kerosene lamp.

"He became aware of an aroma that stirred his memory. He stopped for a moment and sat on the bed feeling light-headed, and looked out beyond the blood-stained floor through the open door. He saw the bay and mountains beyond. The scar on his chest seemed to burn. He got to his feet and brushed the ash and dust off of the piano. He opened the keyboard to see the keys still shiny and even. He opened the top and looked inside. The geometry of wires and hammers was as it should be. He closed the piano and turned to see the sun glint off of a golden framed photograph hanging on the wall over the head of the bed. Even from across the room the lady in the picture seemed to be looking at him, then in another step he was struck that it was her. It was Marie De Paris. Suddenly everything fit together – ladies of the night who knew of the opera, the gift in memory of Marie, the beautiful lady who had killed herself over a lost love, the opera voice they had heard from the *Discovery*…

"He took the photograph off the wall. There was a note written elaborately on the back, 'Paris 1857, My darling Val, If I could again find you, I would never leave you for a moment. All my Love, forever, Marie De Paris.' He sat and watched through the small window as the day wore on and the evening colors softened and led into the night.

"Hecky, Val was definitely in love with Marie, and with Susan, but you will learn there are many kinds of love in this world. I hope you will experience them all as I think Val Baronoffsky did. He kept this photograph his whole life. It is possible for humans to love more than one person at a time. I love you and Bonnie, and I love your mom, and I love the memories your dad left with us, but each is different. Not better or worse, not more or less, just different.

"The next day Val began to add a music room onto the clinic in his house. He hired people to work on it day and night. The room was large and beautiful with carved double doors, fancy window seats, and ceiling beams that matched the dark hardwood trim around the whole room. He moved the piano in and for the rest of his life any child in Seattle that wanted piano lessons could have them at the Marie De Paris room, free. There would be grand Christmas concerts there every year, and after he started a university scholarship program in her name, the recitals and awards were held there.

"The old piano made it possible for at least fifty students to attend the university and thirty-one of them were first introduced to music through the free program. The old piano was played at the party where I met your grandpa. It was a Christmas party and as usual Doctor Baronoffsky invited the family of every patient he ever had treated, and also every new family in Seattle. Hundreds of people would visit the open house. There would be someone playing the piano almost every minute.

"Your grandpa was one of those people who could do no wrong at a keyboard. He and I were just teenagers then and he had just moved to Seattle to attend the university. He was half Nez Perce Indian, and he still allowed his hair to run in a single braid. He had gone to Mission School in Walla Walla, and later in Oregon. He made his way to Seattle by himself to find a job and work his way through the university. He was one of the Seattle newcomers who had heard that he, too, was welcome at Doc Baronoffsky's open house. He played the entire evening. When the party was winding down, your great grandpa offered him a job teaching piano to the students at the free school, and asked him if he would agree to stay in the apartment above the old carriage house. Without that old piano, your grandpa might not have been able to attend the school and become an engineer, and worst of all, we might have never met.

"My favorite memory of the old piano is when your great grandfather played at my wedding. He played a song he had written and my mom sang the accompaniment.

"It was also played at his funeral, by your grandpa and I. The notes carried out the open window of the music room to the people that overflowed the house and filled the front yard and the street beyond. We played a duet he had taught us. It was a piece of music or a poem written in a fine hand. He found it folded in behind the backing of the picture of Marie De Paris. She wrote the poem on light blue paper with tiny roses in each corner. She called it, Once Upon The Tide. Here is how it went:

"I see the sun as it rises there,
I feel the warmth of morning air,
I know this breeze I feel so light,

Will bring you to me tonight.
For it is only in my dreams you live,
It is there I await the love you give.

"I float upon the ocean tide,
Warmth of love fills me inside,
Waves roll and crash and pass me by,
My love for you shall never die.

When darkness comes and the sunset nears,
I will steal away the chilling fears
Of unseen things, and unwept tears,
Of unfilled dreams, of all the years.

"Our love will calm the stormy sea,
And be there to give you strength inside
So please remember this of me,
I give you strength of the ocean tide.

"The piano has been silent since your Dad was killed in the war. I know you remember he also had a gift of music. It is just so hard for your mom and me to imagine someone else playing the old thing. He played for us the night he left, and since then it has not been used."

"But why do you want to get rid of it? Maybe we will never get a chance to get it back again. What if someday I have a family. Do you want me to just help them forget about who they are and that they are as strong as the tide?" I just couldn't see how she could be so proud of the family history and at the same time willing to have my great grandfather's piano hauled off.

"Please try to understand, I don't want to get rid of it," she said. "I cry just to think I could bring myself to do that – the piano is part of me too you know. But, sometimes we need to make difficult choices and things are hard for us now, Hecky. I don't see them getting much better for a long while, and we need to take care of this old house, too. If your dad was still alive, things would be fine, but since we lost him, we have had to get by with a lot less income. We have been able to make things work until now, but the roof has started to leak and we cannot fix that ourselves. Your mom works every day but still we need the extra money to fix the roof before next winter. I'm so sorry things have come to this." I felt like I was making her defend something she didn't want to do. At least now I understood what was going on even though I didn't have a solution.

Adrian sat attentive, holding Hydro. He was dressed with a white shirt and a necktie over a tailored jacket which matched his pants. He said, "Can't work today, rain you know."

Grandma smiled, "You look so nice."

"Thank you. I like to dress this way, perhaps it is my vanity. I keep thinking about the piano. Actually, the piano was on my mind all night. I understand how important it is and how attached to it you are. I don't want to move it, even though I have a buyer who will pay a very good price for it. I think the old piano is a member of your family, and it belongs here, no matter what. I have a rather unusual proposition for you to consider." Grandma refilled his cup, and smiled again.

"In addition to the Atlas Moving Company, I also own the Atlas Roofing Company. I looked at your roof from the street this morning and I would say it is in pretty sound shape except for needing new shakes. They are not hard to put on, though I stopped doing that years ago myself. This is the kind of job some roofers are not eager to do because the roof is quite steep and high. However, during the summer I have a lot of helpers from the university and I need to keep them busy all the time. If they do not work every day they come up short for their tuition. I don't have a scholarship program like the one your father had, but I have helped a few through when they really needed it, if they are good workers.

"As the situation is now, I have an extra crew available for four days. If it is okay with you they can start working here at sunrise tomorrow."

"I don't understand," she said, hands hiding her mouth. She sat down.

"Well it's like this. I recognized long ago the only legacy I can leave for the younger generation is some personal sense of values. The only way I can do that is to show them how life works, or how I think it should work. When you start hearing those roofing tacks going in tomorrow, just think of it as being a return for every time one of Doctor Baronoffsky's free students hit a key. When you see the crew of college students show up and start to crawl all over your roof, just think of all of the college kids your family has one way or another helped through the university. When lunchtime comes and the crew climbs down from the roof and starts to eat on the lawn, just see that the windows are open and the piano gets played. I'll be out there with them, and I want to hear it, too."

"I can't pay you."

"I know." He walked up to her and put his arms around her. She put her head against his chest. I was happy, but embarrassed so I stepped out on the porch, but I could hear them.

"Adrian," she said real quietly, "I have waited for you too long."

"No," he said, "It is never too late to be alive."

CHAPTER 16

Susan

By the end of the week, we had a new shake roof on our house and everything about the roof looked a lot better than the old one. Adrian spared no expense. His crew took all of the old mossy cedar ones off, and replaced them with new shakes he said would last thirty years. He didn't tell Grandma, but I saw the gutters had been replaced along with the roof, and that Adrian's crew had done some work around the chimneys too. The crew was a dozen college-age men, and they flew through the job.

It took three full days, counting the extra long lunches. While the crew ate she sat at the old piano and played the songs she knew as a girl, finishing with three hymns each day. Adrian asked her to play *Rock of Ages* and *Old Rugged Cross*, and the guys sitting on the grass all joined in the singing. Music filtered down the street and echoed between the houses. By the time lunch was done, our neighbors were standing on the grass talking to the men as if they were all guests at the same party.

The roofing was finished near sundown. The crew had packed up their gear and cleaned the place up neater than they had found it. Every one of them filed past Grandma, saying things like, "Sure enjoyed meeting you," or "Thank you for the wonderful food and the music," and "Thanks for letting me help with your roof, God bless you," and so on. She stood on the front porch and shook hands with them all, and remembered all of their names.

The last in line was Adrian. He was dressed in a clean white shirt with the sleeves rolled up, open at the neck. For a guy who said he didn't do roofing any more, he could climb the ladders and walk the steep roof as if it was flat ground. I watched him as he helped the young men, showing them how to fit the shakes and make the roof, "right and tight," as he called it. I could hear him say, "This old house is a fine old thing with many years left. We need to keep the weather out so it can raise more fine families like the ones that have lived here before." From time to time he would drop to his knees and work beside the younger men and talk with them. Sometimes he would go up and down the ladders carrying bundles of shakes, or a jug of cold water for the men on the roof. Other times he would work at a saw that was set up down below to make special cuts. He would let the saw scream and chatter through the shakes, then he would carry his finished work to one of his crew.

It was at the end of the day that he changed into a clean white shirt. He and the other men seemed very pleased with what they had done, and it was clear to me they enjoyed the work and they enjoyed being with each other. The crew piled into the assortment of multi-colored, dented pickups, sat in the beds and hung out the open windows of the cab, waving as they drove out of sight. They seemed to look forward to seeing each other tomorrow, and I knew for a fact they really liked old Adrian.

Grandma and Adrian stood together on the porch and waved after them. Grandma stood close to him and she rested her head against his shoulder. I could see her put her arm around his waist and look up at him. She said something I could not quite hear. He smiled broadly and turned toward her. He was a head taller and so broad she disappeared as he lifted her off her feet and spun her around. I waited for her to say stop it, but she just laughed out loud. Hers was a real rolling laugh, louder and louder. I felt good she was having fun as they danced together on the smooth wood boards of our porch, to some silent music they both heard. Adrian stayed for dinner so I ate quietly then excused myself, I felt a little uncomfortable.

The next morning the rain started. As usual Grandma was already up and working in the kitchen. She had the fire going to take the dampness out of the air. I loved the smell of the kindling as she started the old stove. The crackle of cedar always reminded me of home and her. As I walked in, I heard steps on the rear porch, and through the lace curtain on the kitchen door I could see it was Adrian. She pulled the door open before he knocked.

"Hi, Hecky. How you doin'? Can't start a new roof job on a rainy day. Don't want to take chances one of those young fellows might slide off a customer's roof. Gets pretty slick up on some of 'em you know. Besides if we tear it off the rain will come in and the whole idea is to keep the rain out, right? So, Susan, how would you like to tell me a little more about this family? If you have other plans, no hard feelings." Before she could answer I said, "Great idea. We still need to hear about the Mission, your mom, how we got this old house, what happened to Val and Susan, and did Susan know about Marie De Paris, and..."

She cut me off with a laugh. "Okay, okay, but first you both need to have some breakfast." She was already cooking the meal and I could see she was nearly done. I just watched the rain and waited. The wind began to blow the dimples and splashes across the porch. I was happy we had Adrian around.

He talked while we ate. "Those shakes are real history you know. They came across the sound from the Olympic Peninsula over by Port Angeles. There was a time about eighty five years ago Seattle was a village and the other mill towns were real going concerns. Its not like those other mill towns will die - they will just become so diverse that people who happen on the scene fifty years from now will never guess our heritage. They won't have enough clues to recognize timber towns, and Seattle was the smallest of them all.

"The forest needs time to heal itself. When the trees were cut and made into lumber they were shipped out to other cities, states and countries. The trees of the Pacific Northwest built the world for your generation Hecky. In your lifetime you will see Seattle become an immense city. In the meantime, timber towns which do not change will dry up and disappear."

He smiled at himself, and shifted in his chair, as if he was overdoing it. Grandma was behind him riveted to the floor, holding the coffee pot. I could tell she was wrapped up in what he was saying.

"Well, the shakes we put on this seventy-three-year-old house are from a two-hundred-year-old tree. That tree was twenty-five-years-old when Captain James Cook discovered the Strait of Juan de Fuca. He might have seen it standing there with others for it came from the north slope of the Olympic Mountains overlooking the strait where he set anchor.

"It has always bothered me somewhat to say that anyone actually discovered this place, since all of these so called discoverers were met by Indians who had been here for hundreds of years already, perhaps longer. The great Chief Seattle said, 'People were so numerous at a time before the whites came that they covered the land as the waves of a wind ruffled sea cover its shell paved floor.'"

Grandma checked the oven and came to the table with fresh coffee and hot rolls. She sat down next to Adrian. When he took a bite of the hot, buttered roll she started to talk. "Then the tree that made our roof was one hundred and fifteen years old when Val and Susan Baronoffsky sailed by on their way to the village of Seattle. They also may have seen it there on the slopes of the Olympic Mountains overlooking the strait. It would have been taller than many of the trees around it. Adrian has already told me the tree rings, and the ages of the trees around it, show that there was a forest fire when our tree was about fifty years old. Our tree survived the fire. Hecky, they could have seen this tree and admired it even then, and now it's keeping us warm and dry.

"I know Susan was a woman of passion. She had a passion for the arts and for life itself. She was a woman of deep commitment and understanding. How hard it must have been for her to leave her own culture far behind. She had to change everything she knew, but she was able to change. She even took advantage of the opportunities change extended to her. She not only became a citizen of this new town, but in many ways she became a leading citizen.

"You won't read about her in the history books, perhaps because she was native. At that time there were strong feelings against anything native, and there was no place in Seattle society for the Indians. Today we can look around the city and see how much racial hate there is even now, among the so-called educated people. The parts of our city that are the most prosperous are in a sense the most backward. Hecky, you need to know there are neighborhoods like The Highlands, Windermere, Sand Point, Shoreline, Richmond Beach, Roosevelt, Mountlake Terrace, Lake Forest Park and many others that have nice homes for the well to do and supposedly intelligent leading citizens of our city, but they find ways to keep out minorities even now in 1950. This is the mentality that prevailed when Val and Susan were trying to make a home here in the 1860s.

"When Val and Susan came to the village of Seattle, interracial marriages were unheard of. They were two exceptional people and they won friends and respect because they earned it. They were able to establish themselves in the village but not without incident.

"This old house we are in right now was actually built twice, well, almost twice. When Susan and Val came into what was then the village of Seattle they were an unusual couple. He a handsome, powerful young doctor and she an exotically beautiful, wistful young lady, perhaps the prettiest one around but still very different from the typical pioneer wife. She set herself apart in many ways, some she couldn't help. He, on the other hand, was eagerly welcomed into all social circles.

"When Susan was growing up, remember she spent all of her younger years in the Arctic village where she was born. Everyone there and everything was native in every respect. There was no other culture, few of the native villagers were even vaguely aware that there were other cultures. Their world was limited to them and what they knew. In their place and time, people, men and women alike, were valued for what they were, not what they could appear to be. Respect could only be earned.

"In Seattle society, things seemed to be different, at least among the women. They took great pleasure in meeting and talking about quilts, knitting, pies, and the like. Susan's grasp of the new culture was limited and she found it confusing. She had an excellent grasp of the language and had learned to read and write, which is more than could be said for some of Seattle's leading ladies. She had not run across the kind of hate that intelligence cannot overcome.

"At first her quietness was taken as shyness, then next seen as aloofness, then conceit, then hatefulness. Before Susan could learn about quilts, knitting, and pies, she was no longer welcome anywhere. Suddenly she had become 'that native wife of the new doctor' and people would pass her by on the streets and ignore her in the stores unless she was with Val. Val was accepted and relied on for his advice and knowledge. He was expected to become a civic leader, but as the ladies of the city began to ignore, ostracize, and denigrate Susan, he began to doubt that Seattle was the beautiful place the settlement had seemed to be when they first saw it from the foredeck of the *Discovery*.

"The new house on the hill had been started by the time Val became aware of what he considered to be a serious problem. Susan had said nothing, but Val was no fool. He saw the light within her began to dim, he saw the energy seem to ebb, he saw the ever present interest in things around her begin to fade, and he worried over it. She would not admit there was any kind of problem, for in her mind she did not know what it was. To her, prejudice had not been either a word or an idea.

"It was Old Doc Maynard who told young Doc Baronoffsky what the problem was, as they were treating an old Indian woman for a wound she had received by a white hunter. Old Doc Maynard was an intelligent and perceptive man – and when he wasn't drinking, talkative if not eloquent. 'If anyone could overcome this, Susan would be the one,' he said. 'The world will need people who can be the first ones, and she is one of them. Someday there will be people of every color and mix on this planet, and when Seattle is a big city they will number in the thousands. Like the tide, they will come and go as they like, they will live and work where they please, and they will raise their families to become this cities greatest treasure.

"'But first there will be someone to receive the hate, to be aware of it, to feel the heavy burden and still stand straight. This person will be alone, always alone with their feelings, and therefore must have unlimited inner strength. She must be stronger than all of the hate in everyone, and still be able to be gracious, loving, and peaceful despite what happens, for there is no limit to what can happen.

"'She must deal with the worst of times caused by the darkness that dwells in others. Above all she must be aware of the resentment, recognize it is resentment, and still not harbor hate within herself. Susan may have been sent here to heal this place, to banish the evil, to blaze a trail for others. How is it we are so backward we can invade this place and cast out the people who have lived here so long before us, then have the conceit to treat them as outsiders. Not many people would be able to deal with this in a way things could be made better, but I think she is one. Perhaps she was sent here for this purpose.'

"Many stories persisted about Old Doc Maynard's doings

and among some of the newcomers who arrived with ample bank accounts and old family money from back East, he was viewed as a silly old man. Among the tight knit group of pioneers and adventurers who paid their dues with blood, sweat, and tears, he was a genius. Baronoffsky knew he was hearing the truth.

"For a few moments they worked in silence as Baronoffsky stopped the bleeding and repaired the damage by reconstructing and saving what he could in an environment more suitable to cleaning fish than saving lives. He worked quietly in crude conditions, his fingers gently feeling the damage hidden by torn flesh and oozing tissue. In his mind a picture of the anatomy with all of the intricate networks of veins, arteries, bones, ligaments, and nerves took shape as his fingers examined and explored. His manipulations and stitches stemmed the bleeding and the arm began to look like it belonged to the shoulder from which it had nearly become detached. Color started to returned and the nails again looked alive.

"He comforted and reassured the patient as he worked, quieting her fears that to be a bird with one wing is no better than death itself. He would, he said, have her be 'a woman with two arms that would hold her grandchildren, pick her berries, weave her baskets. Two arms to raise to the morning sun, two arms she could wave to the ocean breeze, two arms with which she could hold her husband.' She did not cry or whimper as he worked. When Baronoffsky was done, Doc Maynard helped close the wound.

Baronoffsky studied the patient closely, making her as comfortable as possible, and reassured the children around her. He gathered them together and began to shepherd them to where he and Susan had set up a temporary home. As Susan talked with each one and made them a hot meal, Baronoffsky took Doc Maynard aside.

"'Sir, earlier you made a profound observation, or perhaps a prophesy. Either way, I take it as a gift of providing me with insight into the future. Although I do not feel you are in need of reassurance, I want you to have the comfort of hearing me say to you that my faith in Susan is complete, total. You can feel assured I am not going to sit here and be an idle spectator to the diminution, subversion, or destruction of human freedom, and neither is she.

"'*We the people,* is a very eloquent beginning. When that document was completed on the 17th of September, 1787, not all of this young nation's people were meant to be included, and I feel that to be morally wrong. To me, all are equal under the eyes of God and so it shall be on earth. I am committed to fairness and equality, and so is she.'

"Susan, making bandages, heard the conversation and she entered the discussion. She knew very little about the Constitution, and little of the principles of government, although thanks to the leather bound books on the *Discovery* she knew more than most of the people of Seattle.

"'I think everyone is different in every way, in size, thought, color, and destiny. The God that put us in this place and time did it with love, giving us a world of our own. But, we do not have control over the world to use and destroy. The world is like one living thing we need to be part of, to nurture, to worship. In the same way the earth is a gift from God, each person is also. It is up to each of us to do what can be done to each other, and for each other, as God would do it.'

"Susan had observed the behavior of the officials at the trade post, and had heard the story about Father Ivanoff. In her mind she was aware there was a presence of evil in some people, but she felt love, understanding and forgiveness could overcome all that. I never knew her to change her thinking.

"The hunting accident happened on the open beach a mile from town where an Indian woman was gathering clams with her grandchildren. They had been warned away from the beach the day before by some newly arrived settlers, but they did not understand, for their families had gathered clams at this place for hundreds of years. The accident had been a warning shot to scare them off, but the settler had instead hit the woman, nearly ruining her arm. She and her grandchildren were trying to walk back to Doc Maynard's when she collapsed into the arms of Doc Baronoffsky at the foot of Skid Road.

"Doc Maynard said, 'This will happen again, and we both know it. The Indians are peaceful here and I love these people, but I have no way to protect them. We are driving them from a place that is theirs, and to which they have every right to keep. We are so far apart I fear their culture will be erased by our so-called progress, and civilization.'

"As Old Doc was talking, the shooter approached the ring of people that had gathered at the bloody scene now taking place in back of Doc Maynard's store. Bulging eyes, cords standing out in his neck, through crooked yellow teeth – 'I warned 'em. How dumb are they? What they come back for? I got a settlement there. Come all the way here from St. Louis and I ain't puttin' up with no squatters on my beach.' Brown liquid dribbled from the corner of his mouth as he hunched, leaning closer to the men in the back of the store, the smell of skunk permeating the room. Nothing was said as Baronoffsky pushed the door open to coax fresher air into the room. Doc Maynard motioned the man outside then closed it silently as the man stepped through, dragging the shotgun behind, shuffling misshapen boots.

"Almost by the day the bitter tide grew. New arrivals to Seattle would be indoctrinated by the group, and in their need to be accepted by the community they would listen. Their silence was taken as agreement and support for the resentment that had become almost the norm among many of the whites, especially the newcomers. Unknowingly Susan had become the center of attention. No matter how striking she was in her appearance, how intelligent and polite she was, she was pointed out as 'the one who is above her station,' 'the uppity one,' 'the one who tries to act white,' 'the fancy squaw,' 'The Siwash woman,' and her presence was called to the attention of every newcomer as an example of what should never be permitted to happen. When not with Val, she was ignored except in Doc Maynard's store, although others would leave hurriedly when she came in. On the board sidewalks, other walkers looked away. There were no invitations, there were no visits.

"The house Val and Susan had started to build was well underway in a matter of weeks, since they were able to hire plenty of help from among the friendlier people in the settlement. It was to be exactly the same as this house, and just about at the same location., and was intended to be the nicest house in the city, if not in the entire territory. Compared to the others around it, even the fashionable Victorians on the hill, it would look like a mansion. Some of the older people were proud that such a fine new home would decorate their city. Others however, couldn't accept that a white man would dare to live there with his native wife.

"They saw the blaze fill the summertime evening sky as they returned from Bainbridge Island, where they had been caring for an Indian boy who was run down by a settler's wagon. The moonlight was bright, the heavens were full of stars and there was a calm on the water, enough almost to allow Susan and Val to escape the turmoil surrounding the young boy. Val and Susan were talking softly to each other as they often did, revealing their thoughts and sharing their feelings, when they saw the flicker of flame from far out in the bay. They knew that all of Seattle, except those paying attention to other things at the saloon, would be asleep. As the flicker rapidly soared into a tower of sparks and flying cinders that lit the hillside, they knew the embers came from their house.

"As their tiny sloop arrived at the city dock, the light of early morning stung their sleepless eyes. They trudged up Skid Road toward the white houses on the hill. A silent group of Seattle society had gathered near the ruins. As they approached, Yesler, Boren, Denny, and others came down the street to meet them. They were apologetic and tearful as they embraced Susan, and offered Val a donation of all the lumber and labor to rebuild the house. They were honest, hard-working and likeable men, but even in their sincere goodness they could not make up for the spirit that had kindled the fire, nor could they quiet the fear in Susan's heart. It was obvious the fire had been started outside intentionally.

"They were kicking through the still hot embers when the bartender of the Mad House Saloon came over with a jug of hot coffee and some sandwiches. He offered his condolences and help in reconstruction. He told them, 'The guys at the mill stopped by the saloon real early this morning and they left a collection of a little cash wrapped in this here hanky. They put their names on a list of people willing to donate labor for building you another house. The list includes everyone on the morning shift of the mill, and that's enough men to build three houses pretty damn quick.'

"'Well, we sure won't need three houses, but someday it might be nice to have enough children to fill three of them up.' The bartender laughed, and Susan blushed.

"She said, 'I would have a thousand children for Val if I could, and every one of them would be loved and cared for just as much as the first and the last.'

"The bartender looked at her. His face softened as he stepped toward her. He extended his arms and curled her into an embrace. 'Susan, Susan, you are a precious creature as loving and intelligent as you are beautiful. How I wish there were more like you.'

"Val smiled at them, and thought *how nice to have real friends.*

"The bartender looked in her eyes and murmured, 'Thanks for being here.'" He turned to Val. 'Thanks for bringing her.'

"He started to walk off, then he turned, 'Oh I forgot to tell you there was a man looking for you at the saloon last night. Said he knew you from the dock at Boston years ago. Left early this morning headed for San Francisco. Asked about some black man named Adam, too.'

"Well, Hecky, Val and Susan used to tell me it was probably a good thing the house was set on fire, because the fire caused them to do some deep thinking about who they were and what they wanted for their own lives. Susan brought it up as they were standing in the ashes, looking out at the bay and the wisp of smoke rising from the Indian settlements on Bainbridge Island. "'Look there Val. See the smoke? This is like a sign to me. I feel like we are being called there for some reason. Seattle has another doctor now, and we can help Doc Maynard equip his hospital, so Seattle will have everything needed for now. Maybe we are not necessary here. Seattle will soon be a city, and the more it grows the harder times will be for the Indian people to survive. They will be driven further and further away until they will not be able to live the Indian ways any longer. They will fade away like the summer fades with the winter cold, only for them there will be no spring. Times will be very hard for them. Food will be harder and harder to get, and white man's sickness will kill many. The people there will know suffering that the people in Seattle will never fathom. What can we do here others cannot do? Do you feel as I do that we can make life easier for those across the way? Do you feel like you are being called there?'

"The grandmother who had suffered the gunshot wound, the young boy who had his legs crushed, the dead people in Tom and Robert's village – they were all still fresh images in Val's mind. They were events that troubled him greatly, and until now he had not understood what they meant for him.

"'Susan you are a magnificent, wonderful, gracious, beautiful woman who I love more than life itself. What you are showing me is what I could not see for myself. We do not need this huge house, not now. Now we need to be over there, and we can camp on the beach if we have to. We will live as they live. Perhaps we can ease the pain, perhaps we can help them deal with change, and perhaps we will be helping ourselves. I feel good right now, and the sadness I had when I saw this house going up in flames is gone.' He had his hands on her shoulders as he looked in her eyes, their noses almost touching.

"Very little was salvageable except the items that had been stored at Doc Maynard's, or piled on top of the piano in the cabin. Val and Susan gave almost all of their new medical equipment to Doc for the new hospital being added onto the back of his store. Susan became Val's nurse, and they camped that summer on the beach at the Indian village. In the fall they built a small cabin on the other side of Bainbridge Island, near a bigger Indian settlement where old Chief Seattle is now buried. The cabin overlooked a pebble beach that opened to a narrow tidal channel. The salt water ran like a river one way on the incoming tide, then reversed itself to run in the other direction when the tide ran out. There were always fish, and the beach out front offered plenty of clams and oysters. The salmon gathered in great schools facing into the current, and always they were large and bright as chrome. They saw orcas there, but now they are gone from this area, just like the Indians.

"That's the place where I was born, in 1877. Can you imagine what a thrill a healthy child must have been to them there. By then, Val was forty-six years old, and Susan was thirty-one. They both wanted a large family, but that wasn't to be.

"In many ways, though, their family was much larger than anyone could count because more than one tribe welcomed them in their council. Many Indian children were raised by them at different stages of their lives, and I know twelve who knew them only as Mother and Father. So you see I was born an only child, but I have a dozen brothers and sisters from three different tribes. I have more aunts, uncles, and cousins than I can count. One way or another we are related to just about every tribe in the Pacific Northwest.

"I have no doubt Val and Susan were very happy there. Theirs was a simple life, but it was probably their happiest time. Their days were basic but good, and removed from the city's growing pains. Every neighbor we had was like family to us. We shared everything. That was the kind of place with a time of its own, and that time has passed onto other frontiers. Life is enough to know such times, and to me, that place has the kind of memories this old house will have for you someday."

I already understood what she was talking about, for I had often thought this could not last forever. She and my mom would leave me behind just like my dad did, and all I would have is memories. I thought about that some when we were told Dad was killed in the war, and again when Grampa died. I had already gathered a lot of great memories, and I liked it most when I could share them with people like Bonnie. She had some, too, and sometimes we would agree to keep a secret. She knew how I felt about my Dad, and I knew she understood.

"Hecky, the house my dad and mom had there on the edge of that pebble beach was just like the one your Grandpa and I built on that bluff above the sandy beach at Bainbridge Island decades later. I know you remember that place, and the fun you used to have there when Grandpa was alive. Keep those memories fresh and treasure them, for someday you may be able to pass them onto someone like I am doing to you, but you can never go back.

"Susan, my mother, liked her life there. This I know, for she spoke of the place often in later years. I think moving there was a relief for her in a way because being in a different place among the Indians took her out of the controversy, and conflict that surrounded them in the city, and put her closer to the Indian people with whom she had a natural link. The adventure was a good thing, for it gave her time to learn and grow, and gave them time to enjoy their love for each other. They were timeless companions in those years, partners in everything.

"Moving over there was good in another way too, a very different way. I think she felt she was in competition with Marie De Paris, who held a place in my dad's heart even after her death. Marie seemed to have a hold over both of them. He could not visit, or even talk of, the cabins behind the Mad

House Saloon, even years after the death of Marie De Paris. My mother and father never talked about Marie, but each year my mother visited Marie's grave marker on the anniversary of her death and placed flowers there. When she was feeling old and tired she once told me she did not hate this woman, but she wished she would have known her. When Marie died she took a bit of my father with her, and my mother lived out her life trying to find ways to get it back.

"We moved back to the city when I was five years old and ready for school. I didn't want to leave. That place was the only world I knew and all my friends were there. It was a child's paradise. Nature was unspoiled. Most of the settlers wanted to be on the side of the bay near Seattle, or near other places that were sure to become big cities. The Indian ways were kept alive there, and as I look back now I can see there are few of the old ways left, even on the reservation. I think the Indian's values were destined to be wiped out when the reservations were created. Chief Seattle spoke of it."

She had picked up one of Val's notebooks from a shelf near the table where we sat, and opened it to the inside of the back cover. She read aloud from something Val wrote that Chief Seattle had said. "'When the last Red Man shall have perished, and the memory of my tribe shall have become a myth among White Men, these shores will swarm with the invisible dead of my tribe, and when your children's children think themselves alone in the field, the store, the shop, upon the highway or in the silence of the pathless woods, they will not be alone. In all the earth there is no place dedicated to solitude. In the night when the streets of your cities and villages are silent and you think them deserted, they will throng with the returning hosts that once filled them and still love this beautiful land. The White Man will never be alone. Let him be just and deal kindly with my people, for the dead are not powerless. Dead did I say? There is no death, only a change of worlds.'

"The reservations were all too small to allow the Indian

way of life to continue, and perhaps the whites planned it that way. There was no real school there, just the one my mother started. She had no formal schooling, but she was intelligent and a hard worker. The school she started was primarily for the Indian children who were denied any other education, but the word soon got around and white settlers began to arrange to have their children attend there too. Most of them lived too far away to let the children travel back and forth each day, so Val and Susan started a boarding school to accommodate them. Mother taught several of the older children to read and write, and Father taught them arithmetic and history, so when we left for the city, the school could be continued by others.

"By that time Seattle even had a fledgling university, so we settled once again in the city. Seattle had four churches, a water system, an assortment of dry good stores, bakeries, stables, blacksmiths, a foundry, plumber and tin shop, surveyors, a millinery, a photography shop, dressmakers, a drug store, a newspaper, and of course a hospital, mills, shippers, hotels, a bank, and the indispensable saloons. My father practiced medicine in Seattle the rest of his life and passed away in 1900 caring for patients during a diphtheria outbreak. Never one to separate himself from his patients, he tended them round-the-clock. He just drove himself too hard, overtired, he couldn't fight it off.

"He built this house when we moved back to Seattle. He started building in 1882, and the day he started, Val and Susan carved their initials in that big old tree with the broken top out back. The day he finished they set the stone monument in the front of the house at the bottom of the stairs. It was a grand undertaking and it did not get finished until 1885. This was the finest house in the city at the time, and is still a grand old lady. It is magnificent, Hecky, and I am glad your dad was able to make it even better than the day my Father finished it. Now we owe our thanks to Adrian, who has made it better once again."

Adrian leaned over her shoulder to fill her coffee cup, and she blushed. I could see, behind Grandma, that Hydro had a mouse cornered by the pantry door, and it was a standoff. Adrian saw them and picked the mouse up by the tail and placed the little guy outside on the porch. I knew the mouse would be out there feasting on Grandma's cheese for a while. Adrian rinsed his hands then scooped Hydro up and sat down opposite Grandma with Hydro in his lap. She sipped the coffee, smiled a thank you, then went on.

"By the time we moved back to Seattle my mother had become a well educated, well read person. Perhaps one of the best educated ladies in the city, thanks to my father. The two of them could have given me a quality education, but what they wanted most for me was to learn good social skills. My mother had disadvantage because she did not understand the culture, even though by that time she had an excellent grasp of the language. She felt ill at ease and uncomfortable by herself in public, especially after the house was burned down.

"She overcame it all in spades, as they say now. She eventually attended the university and graduated at the age of thirty-four. She became a teacher, specialized in teaching the city's disadvantaged children and founded a nonprofit private school for those needing the kind of help public schools could not offer. She became a champion of women's suffrage, a founder of a mission home for elderly homeless seamen, and a noted local artist.

"My parents were deeply in love with each other and shared a glowing mutual respect. When Val died, my mother could hardly bear up under the pain. They had been best friends, like one person, and when he died, some of her died, too. She never recovered from it.

"The winter following his death, she took a trip by herself to the Arctic. Perhaps she was looking for his spirit there, for inside she was still a native and they have a different way of thinking about the dead. She made the trip up north by steamer in the late summer, and when she got there the coming of winter was in the air. She stayed on, and found someone to take her to a village in the direction of the place where she had lived as a child. She wrote to me that she would sit for hours outside and watch the northern lights and listen to the wind bringing in the winter. When the long winter night came and the sea had frozen over, she said goodbye to everyone and left a letter behind for me. She wandered alone out on the sea ice. She never came back.

"In that letter she wrote the poems I recited to you earlier. I have read the letter so many times I have it in my memory. She also wrote, 'You are born of the wind and the tide. You are the result of a man so strong and loyal I cannot bear to be without him. He is part of me, and soon he and I shall be together again. Your life will go on as it must, for you have great things to bring to this world. Among them must be the legacy to all that follow us, that they too are creatures of the wind and the tide, and within them they have the strength of the ocean.'"

She looked like she was going to cry. I think I understood.

CHAPTER 17

The Poems

I was about ten years old when Grandma told me this story. That was fifty five years ago. When I think of Grandma, I can see her and the old neighborhood clearly. There are very few clues of what used to exist around the old house. Once in a while I still go back to visit Seattle and walk the streets from time to time, though even they have changed. Sometimes I find myself there in the evening. I stand and let the traffic buzz by, as the impatient city refuses to take a rest and city dwellers rush about their business. I close my eyes and close out the sounds. My memory can bring me back to the old neighborhood with old smells, sounds, and personalities.

I like visiting in the evening as the shadows grow long and the colors begin to change. I watch as the fog rises from the pavement and the round steel covers in the street vent wisps of steam into the night air. The fog gathers and drifts against concrete walls, weaving itself between light posts and doorways, then spreading to hide wheels, of cars floating past in the ghostly shine of streetlights and convenience stores.

I sit on a stone bench near the park that overlooks Elliot Bay, underneath an old-fashioned lamppost. It illuminates a bus stop, one of a chain of other posts that create pools of light across the wet blacktop, all the way up to the emergency entrance of a hospital. The hospital covers two city blocks.

I have carried Grandma with me through life, and I searched for that kind of wisdom in others. I know now, at this point in my life, grandparents are as unique to life as ten-year-old boys are to grandparents. Grandma gave me a sense of who I was so clearly that I could feel pride growing inside of me as I heard her stories. Decades later I felt her strength when I ran into the stone walls and cold fences that prejudice built. I kept my balance with an inner resolve and am the better for it. I didn't realize it in my growing-up years, but I had a reserve of self esteem that she put in me, all because I had absolutely no doubt I had the power of the tide.

Grandma left behind the poems that her mother, Susan, wrote. There are eight of them. When I visit this place I take the poems with me. Late in the night, alone on the bench, I read them aloud to the bay.

Printed in the United States
77080LV00002B/124